This is a work of fiction. Similarities to real people, places, or events are entirely coincidental.

THE VICTORIAN LADY'S GUIDE TO RESEARCHING AND WRITING A MYSTICAL ROMANCE NOVEL IN THE STYLE OF MARIE CORELLI

First edition. September 13, 2023.

Copyright © 2023 Aster Alderdice.

ISBN: 979-8223711131

Written by Aster Alderdice.

Also by Aster Alderdice

An Inheritance of Love
The Victorian Lady's Guide to Researching and Writing a Mystical
Romance Novel in the Style of Marie Corelli
Idle Moments: The Mesmerising Hours of Victorian Romantic Poetry
Rhapsodomancy Ancient Divination by Poetry Verses

Introduction

Welcome to "The Victorian Lady's Guide to Researching and Writing a Mystical Romance Novel in the Style of Marie Corelli." In this book, we will embark on a journey back to the enchanting Victorian era, where love was a delicate dance and the realm of the mystical intertwined with everyday life. In this introduction, we will lay the groundwork for the rest of the book, providing an overview of what you can expect to learn and achieve as you delve into the world of Victorian romance writing. The Victorian era, spanning from 1837 to 1901, was a time of immense societal change, technological advancements, and romantic idealism. It was an era that saw the rise of the industrial revolution, the expansion of the British Empire, and significant advancements in science, art, and literature. But it was also a time of strict social conventions, where societal norms and expectations greatly influenced the lives of men and women. Romance novels of the Victorian era often explored themes of forbidden love, societal constraints, and the intersection of the supernatural and the everyday. One of the notable authors of this era who mastered the art of mystical romance was Marie Corelli. Known for her captivating storytelling and unique blend of romance and the supernatural, Corelli was a revered figure in Victorian literature. In this book, we will study her works and draw inspiration from her writing style to enhance our own mystical romance novels. Throughout the chapters ahead, we will explore the essential elements of mystical romance, including creating compelling characters, crafting captivating plots, and building a convincing setting in Victorian London. We will also delve into the research required to immerse readers in the Victorian era, including fashion, social etiquette, and historical events. Aspiring writers will find practical guidance on topics such as developing emotional depth in their writing, writing authentic Victorian letters and correspondence, and handling sensitive and controversial topics with grace. We will also discuss the importance of incorporating elements of humor, nature, and suspense to keep readers engaged. For those who dream of publishing their work, we will explore the process of finding an agent, editing and polishing your manuscript, and marketing and promoting your Victorian romance novel in the digital age. Whether you are a seasoned writer or a passionate reader yearning to create your own mystical romance, this book will serve as your guide. Together, let's unlock the secrets of Victorian romance writing and bring this enchanting era to life on the pages of your novel. So, without further ado, let us venture into the magical world of mystical romance in the style of Marie Corelli.

Chapter 1: The Victorian Era: Exploring the Historical Context

The Victorian Era, named after Queen Victoria who reigned from 1837 to 1901, was a time of great social, cultural, and technological transformation in England. With its unique blend of strict social norms, rapid industrialization, and a fascination with the supernatural, the Victorian era provides a rich backdrop for writing a mystical romance novel in the style of Marie Corelli. In this chapter, we will dive deep into the historical context of the Victorian era, examining the key events, social structures, and cultural beliefs that shaped the period. Understanding the nuances of this era is crucial to creating an authentic and immersive world for your readers. First, we will explore the impact of the Industrial Revolution on Victorian society. The advancements in manufacturing and transportation drastically reshaped the cities, economy, and social dynamics of the era. From the rise of the working class to the emergence of new technologies, the Industrial Revolution had a profound influence on people's lives and can be reflected in the setting of your novel. Next, we will delve into the intricate class system of Victorian society. The Victorian era was known for its strict social hierarchy, with the upper class, middle class, and working class each occupying distinct roles and responsibilities. Understanding the dynamics between these classes will help you create believable characters with accurate social interactions and aspirations. We will also explore the role of women in Victorian society. The era was characterized by a prevailing ideology of domesticity, where women were expected to be virtuous, modest, and submissive. However, this era also saw the rise of the women's suffrage movement and the gradual challenging of traditional gender roles. Examining the limitations and aspirations of women in this period will allow you to create strong, resilient, and independent female characters in your novel. Furthermore, we will discuss the prevalent Victorian values and beliefs, including a strong sense of moral righteousness, piety, and an obsession with respectability. These ideals often shaped romantic relationships, courtship rituals, and the expectations placed on individuals. By understanding these values, you can create authentic romantic arcs and explore the conflicts that arise when societal norms collide with individual desires. Lastly, we will explore the cultural fascination with the supernatural during the Victorian era. This era gave birth to the spiritualist movement, with people seeking answers from the realm beyond. From séances to the exploration of mystical phenomena, the Victorian era provided a fertile ground for the inclusion of supernatural elements in your mystical romance novel. By immersing yourself in the historical context of the Victorian era, you will gain valuable insights into the mindset, motivations, and experiences of individuals living during that time. This understanding will inform your storytelling, allowing you to craft engaging and authentic characters, settings, and plotlines that captivate your readers. So, let's embark on a journey to Victorian England and discover the secrets and wonders of this mystical era.

Chapter 2: Marie Corelli: A Master of Mystical Romance

Marie Corelli, born as Mary Mackay in 1855, was a renowned Victorian author known for her captivating mystical romance novels. She was one of the most popular and best-selling authors of her time, captivating readers with her unique blend of romance, mystery, and supernatural elements. In this chapter, we will explore the life and works of Marie Corelli and understand why she became such a master of the genre.

The Life of Marie Corelli

Marie Corelli's early life was filled with struggles and hardships. Born into a middle-class family in London, she faced financial difficulties in her early years. However, her determination to pursue a literary career led her to persevere through challenging circumstances. Corelli began her writing journey by contributing articles and stories to various magazines and journals. She gained recognition for her work, which eventually led her to publish her first novel, "A Romance of Two Worlds," in 1886. The novel became an instant sensation and established Corelli's reputation as a writer of mystical romance.

The Rise to Literary Stardom

Following the success of her debut novel, Corelli went on to write numerous best-selling novels that delved into the realms of the supernatural. Her works often explored themes of fate, destiny, the afterlife, and the power of love. Readers were drawn to her vivid storytelling and the deep emotional connections she created between her characters. Corelli's novels were also known for their social commentary. She used her writing as a platform to critique societal norms and conventions, challenging the rigidity and hypocrisy of the Victorian era. This made her novels not only entertaining but also thought-provoking for her readers.

The Elements of Mystical Romance in Corelli's Work

Marie Corelli's mastery of the mystical romance genre can be attributed to her unique blend of elements that captivated readers. She skillfully combined romance, mystery, supernatural occurrences, and social commentary to create novels that were both engaging and thought-provoking. In her novels, Corelli often introduced supernatural or mystical elements that played a significant role in the development of the plot and the relationships between characters. These elements added an air of intrigue and enchantment to her stories, keeping readers hooked until the very end.

Influence on Future Writers

Marie Corelli's influence on future writers cannot be understated. Her success paved the way for other authors to explore and experiment with the mystical romance genre. Her unique blend of romance, mystery, and the supernatural inspired many authors to create their own stories with similar elements. Her impact on the genre can still be seen today, as contemporary authors continue to write mystical romance novels that draw inspiration from Corelli's groundbreaking work. Her influence on the genre is a testament to her skill as a writer and the timeless appeal of her novels.

Conclusion

Marie Corelli's contribution to the literature of the Victorian era is undeniable. As a master of mystical romance, she created a legacy that continues to inspire and captivate readers to this day. Her ability to blend romance, mystery, and the supernatural in a thought-provoking manner set her apart as a unique and influential voice in Victorian literature. In the next chapter, we will explore the essential elements of mystical romance novels and how they can be incorporated into your own writing.

Chapter 3: Understanding the Elements of Mystical Romance

In this chapter, we will delve into the key elements that make up a mystical romance novel set in the Victorian era. Understanding these elements will help you create a captivating story that blends romance with supernatural elements in a way that transports readers to a world of enchantment and intrigue.

The Power of Love and Destiny

Central to any mystical romance novel is the theme of love and destiny. Love is portrayed as a force that goes beyond societal conventions and rationality, often defying logic and reason. It is a powerful, all-consuming emotion that can transcend time and space. In your Victorian mystical romance novel, the love between your protagonists should be a driving force in their lives, leading them on a journey of self-discovery and transformation. Their connection should be so strong that it feels destined, as if it was written in the stars.

The Supernatural and Magical Elements

Mysticism and the supernatural play a significant role in a mystical romance novel. This can range from subtle hints of magic to full-blown supernatural occurrences. These elements add an air of mystery and enchantment, providing a backdrop for the unfolding romance. Consider incorporating elements such as secret societies, mythical creatures, or paranormal abilities in your Victorian mystical romance. Be sure to research the popular beliefs and myths of the era to add authenticity and depth to your mystical elements.

Conflict and Tension

Every good romance needs conflict and tension to drive the narrative forward. In a mystical romance novel, this conflict can be intensified by the supernatural elements at play. Perhaps your protagonists come from rival magical families or face opposition from society due to their involvement with the mystical. The tension should keep readers on the edge of their seats, wondering if love will prevail in the face of adversity. It should also create a sense of urgency and stakes that heighten the emotional impact of the story.

Suspense and Intrigue

To keep readers engaged, it's important to incorporate suspense and intrigue into your Victorian mystical romance. This can be achieved through the use of mysterious events, unexpected twists, and hidden secrets. Consider weaving a web of intrigue around your characters, involving them in a larger mystery that deepens the sense of enchantment and wonder. This will keep readers guessing and eagerly turning the pages to uncover the truth.

The Power of Emotions

Emotions are at the heart of any romance novel, and in a mystical romance, they are infused with a touch of magic. The emotions felt by your characters should be powerful, intense, and transformative. Love should be portrayed as a force capable of breaking barriers, healing wounds, and transforming lives. Additionally, emotions such as fear, longing, and desire can be heightened by the mystical elements, adding depth and complexity to the story. By understanding and incorporating these key elements of mystical romance into your Victorian novel, you can create a story that is both captivating and immersive. The next chapter will focus on creating compelling characters that will bring your mystical romance to life.

Chapter 4: Creating Compelling Characters

In a mystical romance novel set in the Victorian era, creating compelling characters is essential to capturing the readers' hearts and immersing them in your story. These characters will drive the plot forward, evoke emotions, and bring your mystical world to life. In this chapter, we will explore the key elements of crafting memorable and engaging characters for your Victorian romance novel.

Understanding Character Archetypes

Before delving into the creation process, it's important to understand the different character archetypes commonly found in mystical romance novels. These archetypes serve as a guide and can help you shape and develop your characters. Some popular archetypes include: 1. The Determined Heroine: A strong-willed and independent woman who defies societal norms and embarks on a journey of self-discovery and love. 2. The Mysterious Hero: A handsome and enigmatic man with a tragic past, who possesses supernatural abilities and carries a deep secret. 3. The Wise Mentor: An older and experienced character who guides and supports the heroine on her quest, providing valuable knowledge and assistance. 4. The Villainous Antagonist: A formidable and cunning character who opposes the hero and heroine's quest, creating conflicts and obstacles along the way. 5. The Quirky Sidekick: A loyal and humorous companion to the heroine, offering comic relief and aiding her in overcoming challenges.

Creating Multidimensional Characters

To ensure your characters resonate with readers, it's crucial to develop them as multidimensional individuals. Here are some tips to bring depth and complexity to your characters: 1. Background and History: Create a backstory for each character, exploring their upbringing, family history, and past experiences. This will influence their motivations, fears, and desires. 2. Flaws and Vulnerabilities: No character is perfect. Give your characters flaws or vulnerabilities that make them relatable and human. These imperfections can enhance character growth and add depth to their journey. 3. Motivations and Goals: Determine what drives your characters. What are their ultimate goals, and why do they want to achieve them? Understanding their motivations will inform their actions and choices throughout the story. 4. Conflicts and Contradictions: Explore internal conflicts within your characters. Perhaps they have conflicting desires or values that create tension and add complexity to their personality. 5. Relationships and Chemistry: Pay attention to the interactions between characters. Create compelling relationships, whether it's romantic, platonic, or antagonistic, with chemistry and tension. These dynamics can further drive your story forward.

Bringing Characters to Life through Dialogue and Actions

Dialogue is a powerful tool for revealing character traits and personalities. Pay attention to speech patterns, word choices, and syntax to differentiate your characters' voices. Additionally, the actions of your characters can also reveal important aspects of their personalities. Show their strengths, weaknesses, and emotions through their behavior and mannerisms.

Research and Authenticity

As your characters inhabit the Victorian era, it's essential to conduct thorough research to ensure authenticity. Familiarize yourself with societal norms, language, clothing, and customs of the time. This knowledge will help you portray your characters realistically and immerse readers in the Victorian setting. Remember, compelling characters are the heart and soul of your mystical romance novel. Invest time and effort into their creation, giving them depth, flaws, and aspirations that readers can relate to and care about. By crafting multidimensional characters, your story will come alive, and readers will be captivated by their journeys and relationships. Let's move on to Chapter 5: Crafting a Captivating Plot.

Chapter 5: Crafting a Captivating Plot

In a Victorian mystical romance novel, a captivating plot is the backbone that keeps readers engaged and wanting to turn the page. It should be filled with intrigue, mystery, and love, while also incorporating the supernatural elements that define the genre. Here, we will explore the key elements of crafting a captivating plot and provide tips on how to create a story that will enchant your readers.

Understanding the Structure of a Mystical Romance Plot

A well-crafted plot is essential to keep readers engaged from the beginning to the end of your novel. While there is no one-size-fits-all formula for a mystical romance plot, there are certain elements that commonly appear in this genre: 1. Introduction: Set the stage by introducing the main characters, the setting, and the conflict or mystery that will drive the story forward. In a mystical romance novel, this could be the meeting of the hero and heroine or the discovery of a mysterious artifact. 2. Rising Action: Develop the plot by introducing obstacles, challenges, and conflicts that the characters must overcome. This may involve their personal struggles, external threats, or uncovering the secrets of the supernatural world. 3. Romance and Mystery: Weave the themes of romance and mystery throughout the plot, ensuring a delicate balance between the two. Every romantic moment should also further the mystery or provide a clue for uncovering the supernatural elements of the story. 4. Climax: Build up tension and suspense until reaching the climax of the story. This is the turning point where the main conflict is resolved, secrets are revealed, and the destiny of the characters is determined. 5. Conclusion: Wrap up loose ends and provide a satisfying resolution for both the romance and the mystery. Leave readers with a sense of fulfillment and closure, but also leave room for potential sequels or spin-offs.

Tips for Crafting a Captivating Plot

Crafting a captivating plot requires careful planning and attention to detail. Here are some tips to help you build a compelling story: 1. Create a Strong Opening: Grab your readers' attention from the first page by setting a tone of mystery and intrigue. Consider starting with an attention-grabbing scene that introduces the conflict or a hint of the supernatural elements to come. 2. Develop a Clear Conflict: Every plot needs a central conflict that drives the story forward. It could be a personal struggle, a mysterious event, or an external threat. Make sure the conflict is well defined and compelling, and that it ties into the romance and supernatural elements of the story. 3. Use Foreshadowing: Hint at the supernatural elements and mysteries throughout the story to create anticipation and keep readers engaged. Foreshadowing can be done through subtle clues, dreams, or eerie coincidences that hint at the secrets and twists to come. 4. Introduce Twists and Surprises: Keep your readers on their toes by incorporating unexpected twists and surprises into the plot. These moments of revelation can create a sense of exhilaration and excitement while ensuring that the story doesn't become predictable. 5. Pace the Story Appropriately: Pay attention to the pacing of your plot, balancing moments of intensity and action with quieter, reflective scenes. Make sure to give your readers time to process information and connect with the characters before diving into another thrilling event. 6. Maintain a Sense of Suspense: Build tension and suspense throughout the story by delaying the resolution of conflicts and unveiling the secrets gradually. This will keep readers invested in the outcome and eager to uncover the final revelations. 7. Create Subplots: Incorporate secondary storylines and subplots to add depth and complexity to your plot. These can explore the relationships and conflicts between supporting characters, add layers to the main conflict, or introduce additional supernatural elements. 8. Use Symbolism and Imagery: Infuse your plot with symbolic elements and vivid imagery to enhance the mystical atmosphere of your story. Symbolism can add depth and meaning to the plot, while imagery can immerse readers in the Victorian setting and the supernatural world. By crafting a captivating plot that seamlessly blends romance, mystery, and the supernatural, you can transport your readers to the enchanting world of Victorian England. Allow your imagination to run wild, and watch as your plot unfolds to captivate and enthrall readers until the very end. Next Chapter:

Chapter 6: Building the Setting: Victorian London

Chapter 6: Building the Setting: Victorian London

In a mystical romance novel set in the Victorian era, the setting plays a crucial role in creating an immersive world for the readers. Victorian London, with its bustling streets, foggy alleyways, and grand architecture, offers the perfect backdrop for a story filled with intrigue, romance, and the supernatural. When building the setting of Victorian London, it is essential to immerse yourself in extensive research to accurately depict the city during that time period. Here are some key aspects to consider when creating the setting for your mystical romance novel:

The Streets of London

Victorian London was known for its maze of streets, filled with a mix of grand avenues and narrow, dimly lit alleyways. The city bustled with activity, from horse-drawn carriages traversing the cobblestone streets to vendors selling their wares on the crowded sidewalks. Describing the sights, sounds, and smells of the streets can help transport the readers into the heart of Victorian London.

The Architecture

Victorian London was characterized by its iconic architecture, ranging from the grandeur of Buckingham Palace to the intricate details of Gothic Revival churches. Descriptions of the city's iconic landmarks, as well as the rowhouses and tenements where the characters reside, can paint a vivid picture of the setting. Pay attention to the architectural styles prevalent during the era, such as Neoclassical, Gothic Revival, and Queen Anne.

The Atmosphere

Victorian London was often shrouded in a veil of fog, which added an air of mystery and intrigue to the city. The fog, along with the smoky chimneys and gas lamps, created a unique and atmospheric setting. Describing the atmospheric conditions and the impact they have on the characters and their surroundings can evoke a sense of suspense and foreboding.

The Neighborhoods

Victorian London was divided into various neighborhoods, each with its own distinct character and social makeup. From the elegant streets of Mayfair, home to the wealthy elite, to the poverty-stricken slums of the East End, the neighborhoods you choose can reflect the social dynamics of the time. Researching the different neighborhoods and their characteristics will help you create a realistic setting that embodies the diversity of Victorian London.

The Underworld

Victorian London had a dark underbelly, with its criminal underworld, opium dens, and secret societies. Incorporating the shadowy side of the city into your setting can add depth and intrigue to your story. Whether it's a mysterious organization plotting in the depths of a hidden lair or a protagonist navigating the dangerous backstreets, exploring the underbelly of Victorian London can create suspense and tension.

Mixing Fiction with Reality

While it's important to accurately depict Victorian London, don't be afraid to mix in elements of fiction and fantasy. The mystical romance genre allows for the infusion of supernatural and magical elements into the setting. Perhaps there are hidden portals or enchanted objects scattered throughout the city, just waiting to be discovered by your characters. Combining the historical reality with fantastical elements can create a unique and engaging setting for your mystical romance novel. Building the setting of Victorian London requires extensive research and attention to detail. By incorporating the intricacies of the streets, architecture, atmosphere, neighborhoods, and the dark underbelly of the city, you can create a vivid and immersive world for your readers to explore. As the story unfolds, the setting will play a significant role in transporting readers back in time to experience the magic and romance of the Victorian era. So, grab your pen and delve into the enchanting streets of Victorian London, where love and mystery await at every corner.

Chapter 7: Researching Victorian Fashion and Style

In a mystical romance novel set in the Victorian era, the fashion and style of the time period play a significant role in creating an immersive and authentic setting. Victorian fashion was characterized by its elegance, intricacy, and attention to detail, and understanding the fashion trends and norms of the era is essential for writing a compelling novel.

Researching Victorian Fashion

To accurately depict Victorian fashion in your novel, it is important to conduct thorough research. Here are some key areas to focus on:

1. Silhouette and Clothing Styles

During the Victorian era, fashion underwent several changes, and each period had its distinctive silhouette and clothing styles. The early Victorian era saw women wearing wide skirts with multiple petticoats and corsets that emphasized a tight waist. As the era progressed, the silhouette became slimmer with the introduction of the bustle, a padded undergarment that added volume to the back of the skirt. Research and study the different wardrobe pieces that women and men wore during this time period. Consider including details about dresses, jackets, trousers, waistcoats, coats, and accessories such as gloves, hats, and parasols.

2. Fabrics and Materials

Victorian clothing was known for its luxurious fabrics and materials. Research the types of fabrics that were commonly used during the era, such as satin, silk, velvet, and lace. Each fabric had its own connotations and was associated with different social classes. The choice of fabric can be used to convey the character's status and personality.

3. Colors and Patterns

Colors and patterns were an important aspect of Victorian fashion. Dark and rich colors such as deep burgundy, navy blue, and emerald green were popular, especially for formal occasions. However, lighter colors like pastels and whites were also worn during daytime events and summer seasons. Patterns such as floral, paisley, and stripes were commonly used, and specific patterns had symbolic meanings. For instance, the use of roses in a pattern symbolized love, while plaids were associated with Scottish heritage.

4. Accessories and Hairstyles

Accessories played a crucial role in completing a Victorian outfit. Women often wore gloves, necklaces, brooches, earrings, and tiaras, depending on the occasion. Men accessorized with pocket watches, tie pins, and cufflinks. Hairstyles for women varied throughout the era, from intricate updos to softly curled styles. Research the popular hairstyles and hair accessories of the time to accurately depict the characters in your novel.

Using Fashion and Style in Your Writing

Once you have conducted thorough research on Victorian fashion, it's time to incorporate this knowledge into your writing. Here are some tips for using fashion and style effectively in your mystical romance novel: - Use clothing descriptions to establish characters and their social status. What a character wears can provide insight into their personality, background, and aspirations. - Pay attention to the details. Describe the cut, fabric, color, and patterns of the clothing to create a vivid image in the reader's mind. - Consider the practicality of the clothing. Victorian fashion often restricted movement, especially for women. Incorporate the physical sensations and challenges characters may face due to their clothing choices. - Use fashion as a means of expression or rebellion. Characters may embrace or reject societal norms through their fashion choices, allowing for character development and conflict. - Show the evolution of fashion throughout the story. The characters' clothing choices can reflect their growth, changing circumstances, or influence on others around them. By carefully researching and incorporating Victorian fashion and style into your mystical romance novel, you will transport readers into the enchanting world of the Victorian era, captivating their imagination and enhancing the overall reading experience.

Chapter 8: The Language of Love: Victorian Romance and Courtship

In the Victorian era, courtship and romance were governed by a set of strict rules and rituals. Love was often seen as a delicate dance, with each step carefully choreographed to adhere to societal expectations. Understanding the language of love in this time period is essential for creating authentic and captivating romantic relationships in your mystical romance novel.

1. Courtship and Marriage

Victorian courtship was a formal process that followed a specific sequence of events. It began with an introduction through a mutual acquaintance or a formal introduction at a social gathering. After the introduction, the couple would engage in a series of supervised meetings to get to know each other better. These meetings were often limited to public spaces and chaperoned by family members or close friends. Once a mutual attraction was established, the man would seek permission from the woman's father or guardian to formally court her. The father's consent was crucial and reflected the importance of family approval in Victorian society. If permission was granted, the couple would enter into a period of courtship, during which they would spend more time together and get to know each other on a deeper level. Engagements were considered a binding commitment, and breaking off an engagement was highly frowned upon. Therefore, the decision to become engaged was not taken lightly. Once the couple was engaged, wedding plans would be made, and a formal announcement would be made in the newspaper.

2. Love Letters and Correspondence

In a time before instant messaging and text messages, love letters were an essential part of romantic communication in the Victorian era. Letter writing was seen as a way to express one's deepest feelings and emotions, and it offered a sense of intimacy and privacy that in-person conversations lacked. When writing love letters, Victorians favored flowery language and poetic expressions of love. They would often use romantic metaphors and draw upon symbols of love, such as flowers and nature, to convey their feelings. Love letters were written with meticulous care, with attention given to the handwriting, choice of ink, and the quality of paper. To add an air of mystery and preserve discretion, lovers would sometimes use a secret code or a specific flower language to convey their true feelings without explicitly stating them. For example, the gift of a red rose symbolized passionate love, while a white rose signified purity and innocence.

3. Social Etiquette and Manners

Social etiquette and manners played a significant role in Victorian courtship. Men were expected to be respectful and chivalrous, while women were expected to be modest and demure. Politeness and good behavior were highly valued, and breaches of etiquette were seen as major social faux pas. During courtship, couples were expected to adhere to strict rules of conduct. Physical contact was limited, with hand-holding being considered the most intimate form of touch in public. Public displays of affection were not encouraged and were seen as inappropriate. Additionally, conversations between couples were expected to be light-hearted and avoid controversial or scandalous topics. Respect for elders and authority figures was also emphasized, and couples were expected to seek the approval and blessings of their families and the community.

4. Symbolism in Romantic Gestures

Victorians were known for their love of symbolism, and romantic gestures were no exception. Small, thoughtful gestures held great meaning and were often laden with symbolism. For example, the gift of a bouquet of flowers carried different meanings depending on the type of flowers and their colors. Victorian couples also expressed their love through the exchange of small tokens, such as lockets with a strand of hair or a piece of jewelry. These tokens were seen as a symbol of commitment and were cherished as precious mementos. Incorporating these symbolic gestures into your mystical romance novel can add depth and meaning to your characters' relationships, creating a more captivating and immersive reading experience. As you write your mystical romance novel set in the Victorian era, remember to pay attention to the nuances of courtship and romance during this time. By understanding the language of love in the Victorian era and incorporating it into your storytelling, you can create rich and authentic romantic relationships that will enchant your readers.

Chapter 9: Unveiling the Mystical: Exploring Supernatural and Magical Elements

In a Victorian mystical romance novel, the inclusion of supernatural and magical elements can add an enchanting layer of intrigue and wonder to the story. These elements evoke a sense of mystery and excitement, captivating readers as they delve into a world where the ordinary meets the extraordinary. In this chapter, we will explore various ways to incorporate supernatural and magical elements into your novel, creating a captivating and immersive reading experience.

Creating a World of Magic

When introducing supernatural and magical elements into your Victorian romance novel, it is important to develop a coherent and believable world of magic. Consider the rules and limitations of your magical system, as well as the source and types of magical abilities present in your story. This will allow you to maintain consistency and prevent any inconsistencies or plot holes. Think about the origin of magic within your story and how it intertwines with the Victorian era. Perhaps there is a hidden society of witches or sorcerers, or maybe ancient artifacts hold mystical powers. Whichever route you choose, ensure that the magic is seamlessly integrated into the historical setting, enriching the narrative rather than overwhelming it.

Supernatural Beings and Creatures

The Victorian era saw a fascination with the supernatural, making it the perfect backdrop for the inclusion of mythical creatures and supernatural beings. Consider introducing creatures such as fairies, vampires, werewolves, or ghosts into your story. These beings can add an air of mystery and danger, heightening the tension and captivating your readers. When depicting supernatural beings, pay attention to their characteristics and how they interact with the human characters in your novel. Create a balance between their mystical nature and their relatability, allowing readers to form emotional connections with these extraordinary beings.

Magical Artifacts and Objects

Magical artifacts and objects can serve as powerful plot devices in your Victorian mystical romance novel. These items hold hidden powers and secrets, driving the story forward and adding an element of adventure and discovery. Consider incorporating artifacts such as enchanted jewelry, mystical books, or ancient relics that possess transformative abilities. The introduction of magical objects allows for exciting quests and challenges for your characters. These objects can be sought after by both protagonists and antagonists, creating a sense of urgency and conflict. Use vivid and detailed descriptions to bring these magical artifacts to life, igniting your readers' imagination and drawing them deeper into the mystical world you've created.

Rituals and Spells

Rituals and spells provide a means for characters to tap into the supernatural powers within your Victorian mystical romance novel. These rituals can range from simple incantations to elaborate ceremonies, depending on the magnitude of the desired outcome. Incorporate rituals and spells strategically throughout your story, using them to advance the plot or deepen the bond between characters. Research the Victorian era's interest in spiritualism and occult practices to find inspiration for your mystical rituals and spells. Consider incorporating elements such as seances, tarot readings, or the use of divination tools. By grounding your mystical elements in the cultural practices of the time, you create a sense of authenticity and immersion for your readers.

Weaving Mystical Elements into the Narrative

Once you have developed the magical aspects of your Victorian romance novel, it is crucial to weave them seamlessly into the narrative. The supernatural and magical elements should enhance the story without overpowering the romance or detracting from the historical setting. Here are a few tips to achieve this balance:

Mysterious Events and Phenomena

Introduce mysterious events and phenomena that spark curiosity and intrigue within the narrative. These supernatural occurrences could be unexplained happenings, prophetic dreams, or strange coincidences. Be mindful of how these events unfold and their impact on the characters and their relationships. By intertwining these mystical elements with the plot, you create suspense and heighten the emotional stakes.

The Influence of Magic on Relationships

Explore the transformative power of magic in relationships and emotions. How does the presence of supernatural or magical abilities affect the dynamics between characters? Do these mystical elements amplify or challenge the romantic bond? Consider the consequences of using magic and how it shapes character growth and decisions throughout the story.

Magic as a Symbolic Element

Utilize symbolism to enhance the narrative of your Victorian mystical romance novel. Infuse magical elements with deeper meaning and significance, connecting them to broader themes of love, destiny, or personal growth. By using magic as a symbolic tool, you add layers of depth to your storytelling, making it more engaging and thought-provoking for readers.

Conclusion

Integrating supernatural and magical elements into your Victorian mystical romance novel opens a world of possibilities for storytelling. Creating a coherent and immersive world of magic, featuring supernatural beings, magical artifacts, rituals, and spells, allows readers to be transported to an enchanting Victorian era filled with mystery and wonder. By weaving mystical elements seamlessly into your narrative, you deepen the emotional impact and engage readers on a profound level. Through mysterious events, the influence of magic on relationships, and the use of symbolism, you can create a captivating and unforgettable mystical romance novel that will transport readers to a world where love and magic intertwine.

Chapter 10: Establishing the Mood: Using Symbolism and Imagery

Symbolism and imagery are essential tools for creating a captivating and immersive reading experience in a Victorian mystical romance novel. By carefully selecting and employing these literary devices, you can establish the mood of your story, deepen the emotional impact, and engage readers on a deeper level.

The Power of Symbolism

Symbolism allows you to convey abstract ideas and emotions through tangible objects, actions, or imagery. In a Victorian mystical romance novel, symbolism can be used to add depth to the story and create a sense of mystery and intrigue. Here are some tips for effectively using symbolism: 1. Select meaningful symbols: Choose symbols that have a strong connection to the themes and motifs of your novel. For example, roses can symbolize love and passion, while a full moon can represent transformation and mystery. 2. Establish consistent symbolism: When introducing a symbol, be consistent in its representation throughout the story. This helps readers understand the deeper meaning behind the symbol and creates a sense of cohesion in your narrative. 3. Use symbolism sparingly: While symbolism can enhance your storytelling, it's important not to overload your novel with too many symbols. Select a few key symbols that carry significant meaning and use them strategically to create impact. 4. Allow room for interpretation: Symbolism is open to interpretation, so leave room for readers to draw their own conclusions. This can spark engaging discussions and make your novel more thought-provoking.

Imagery: Painting a Vivid Picture

Imagery refers to the use of descriptive language that appeals to the senses, allowing readers to visualize the scenes and settings in your novel. By painting a vivid picture with your words, you can transport readers to the Victorian era and create an immersive reading experience. Here are some tips for using imagery effectively: 1. Appeal to the senses: Describe sights, sounds, smells, tastes, and textures to engage readers' senses and bring your Victorian mystical romance world to life. For example, describe the scent of roses wafting through a moonlit garden, or the sound of horse hooves clattering on cobblestone streets. 2. Use vivid and evocative language: Choose descriptive words and phrases that evoke strong imagery. Instead of simply saying "the room was dark," try "the room was shrouded in an inky blackness, with only a flickering candle casting long shadows on the peeling wallpaper." 3. Show, don't tell: Instead of explicitly stating emotions or characteristics, use imagery to show them. For example, instead of saying "she was sad," describe her tear-streaked face and the heaviness in her heart. 4. Create sensory contrasts: Contrast can add depth and complexity to your imagery. For instance, describe a grand ballroom with dazzling chandeliers and opulent decorations, then juxtapose it with the haunting silence of a forgotten attic. 5. Use figurative language: Metaphors, similes, and other types of figurative language can add depth and richness to your imagery. For example, you could compare a character's eyes to twinkling stars, or describe a stormy night as a tempestuous sea. By using symbolism and imagery effectively in your Victorian mystical romance novel, you can establish the mood, create a rich and immersive world, and engage readers on an emotional and sensory level. These powerful tools will add depth and enchantment to your story, making it an unforgettable reading experience.

Chapter 11: Writing Convincing Dialogue

Dialogue plays a crucial role in any novel, and in a mystical romance set in the Victorian era, it becomes even more important. Engaging and convincing dialogue can bring characters to life and enhance the overall reading experience. This chapter will explore tips and techniques for writing convincing dialogue that is authentic to the Victorian era while capturing the essence of a mystical romance.

Understanding Victorian Language and Communication

Before diving into writing dialogue, it is essential to have a solid understanding of how people communicated during the Victorian era. Language and communication styles were quite different compared to modern times. Here are some key elements to consider:

Formality:

Victorian language tended to be more formal and polite. Characters, especially those from the upper class, would use honorific titles and respectful speech.

Vocabulary:

Incorporating Victorian vocabulary can add authenticity to your dialogue. Research common phrases, idioms, and slang used during the era. This research will help you ensure that your characters speak realistically and reflect their social status.

Etiquette:

Victorian society valued manners and proper etiquette. Characters should address each other with proper titles, such as "Sir" or "Madam." The use of "please" and "thank you" was common to display politeness.

Indirect Communication:

Victorian society placed importance on subtlety and modesty. Characters may use more indirect and circumspect language, often relying on innuendos or coded messages to convey their true feelings.

Developing Unique Voices

Each character in your mystical romance novel should have a distinct voice that reflects their personality, social background, and experiences. To create convincing dialogue, keep the following in mind:

Character Background:

Consider your character's upbringing, education, and social status. A working-class character may have a different dialect and vocabulary compared to someone from the upper class. Incorporate these nuances into their speech patterns.

Personality Traits:

Characters with different personalities will express themselves differently. An introverted character may hesitate or use fewer words, while an extroverted character may be more verbose or expressive. Ensure that the dialogue matches their individual traits.

Motivations and Goals:

The motivations and goals of your characters will influence their dialogue. A character driven by revenge may speak with anger and determination, while a character motivated by love may speak with tenderness and passion. Reflect these motivations in their speech.

Conflict and Tension:

Dialogue can be used to heighten conflict and tension between characters. Consider employing verbal sparring, veiled threats, or clever wordplay to create dynamic interactions and keep readers engaged.

Writing Engaging Dialogue

To make your mystical romance novel come alive, follow these tips for writing engaging dialogue:

Show, Don't Tell:

Rather than simply telling readers what the characters are feeling or thinking, show it through their dialogue. Use subtext, hidden meanings, and non-verbal cues to add depth and complexity to conversations.

Avoid Exposition:

Dialogue should not be used as a means to convey information to readers directly. Instead, use it to reveal character traits, advance the plot, or create emotional impact. Information can be more subtly integrated into the narrative.

Keep it Concise:

Victorian language tends to be more flowery and elaborate, but it is important to balance that with brevity. Keep dialogue concise and focused to maintain the reader's attention and pacing of the story.

Use Dialogue Tags Sparingly:

While it is important to attribute dialogue to specific characters, avoid using repetitive or excessive dialogue tags such as "he said" or "she replied." Instead, use action beats or descriptive cues to indicate who is speaking.

Read Aloud:

To ensure that your dialogue flows naturally and sounds convincing, read it aloud. This will help you identify any awkward phrasing, inconsistencies, or unnatural speech patterns.

Exercise: Writing Convincing Victorian Dialogue

To practice writing convincing Victorian dialogue, consider the following exercise: 1. Choose two or more characters from your novel. 2. Imagine a conversation between them that reveals their personalities, motivations, or conflicts. 3. Write the dialogue, paying attention to the Victorian language and communication style. 4. Read the dialogue aloud to ensure it sounds natural and captures the essence of the era. 5. Revise and refine the dialogue as needed, making it more engaging and true to the characters. Remember, writing convincing dialogue is a skill that improves with practice. By incorporating authentic Victorian language and communication styles, developing unique character voices, and following the tips provided, you can create engaging conversations that bring your mystical romance novel to life.

Chapter 12: Developing Emotional Depth in Your Writing

Emotions are the lifeblood of any story, and in a mystical romance novel set in the Victorian era, they take on an even greater significance.

The readers should be able to feel the depth of the characters' emotions and become emotionally invested in their journey. Here are some tips for developing emotional depth in your writing:

1. Show, Don't Tell

Instead of simply telling the readers what the characters are feeling, show it through their actions, dialogue, and body language. For example, instead of saying "She was devastated," you can describe her trembling hands, tear-stained face, and quivering voice to convey her emotional state. By allowing readers to experience the emotions firsthand, you create a more immersive and engaging reading experience.

2. Use Sensory Details

Incorporate sensory details to heighten the emotional impact of your writing. Describe the sights, sounds, scents, tastes, and textures that evoke specific emotions. For instance, if a character is experiencing love and longing, you can describe the soft touch of a lover's hand, the scent of roses in the air, or the taste of a bittersweet kiss. By appealing to the readers' senses, you create a visceral and emotional connection to the story.

3. Explore Internal Monologues

Internal monologues provide a window into a character's thoughts and feelings. Allow your characters to reflect on their emotions and inner struggles. By delving into their fears, desires, and insecurities, you create depth and complexity in their emotional journey. Internal monologues also offer an opportunity to convey the nuances and conflicts within a character's psyche, allowing readers to empathize with their experiences at a deeper level.

4. Utilize Dialogue and Conflict

Dialogue can be a powerful tool for depicting emotional depth. Through conversations, characters can reveal their fears, vulnerabilities, and desires. Use dialogue to create tension and conflict, as well as to showcase the emotional dynamics between characters. Conflict, whether internal or external, can drive character growth and elicit strong emotional responses from both the characters and the readers.

5. Emotional Arcs and Character Development

Every character should have their emotional arc, a transformation or progression in their emotional state throughout the story. Explore the highs and lows of their emotions, allowing them to experience joy, heartbreak, passion, and resilience. Emotional depth comes from the growth and development of characters as they navigate challenges, face their fears, and overcome obstacles. It is through these emotional arcs that readers can connect with characters on a profound level.

6. Balance and Contrast Emotions

Effective storytelling often involves a balance between different emotions. Contrast moments of joy with moments of sorrow, moments of love with moments of conflict. By juxtaposing emotions, you create complexity and depth in your storytelling. This balance can also highlight the contrasts in the characters' experiences, showcasing their emotional journey in a more nuanced way.

In conclusion

Developing emotional depth in your writing is crucial for a mystical romance novel set in the Victorian era. By showing emotions through actions, using sensory details, exploring internal monologues, using dialogue and conflict, focusing on emotional arcs, and balancing contrasting emotions, you can create a rich and evocative reading experience. Tap into the depths of your characters' emotions and let them guide your story, captivating readers and immersing them in a world of love, magic, and intrigue.

Chapter 13: Writing Authentic Victorian Letters and Correspondence

Victorian society placed a strong emphasis on written correspondence, making letters an essential means of communication during this era. In a mystical romance novel set in the Victorian era, incorporating authentic and evocative letters can add depth and realism to the story. This chapter will guide you on how to write authentic Victorian letters and correspondence in your novel.

The Importance of Handwritten Letters

During the Victorian era, letter writing was not only a practical means of communication but also a social ritual and an art form. Handwritten letters held a significant place in society and were cherished as a personal and intimate connection between individuals. By understanding the importance of letters, you can effectively capture their essence in your mystical romance novel.

Structure and Language of Victorian Letters

To write authentic Victorian letters, it is crucial to understand the structure and language commonly used during this time period. Victorian letters followed a specific format and often included specific phrases and conventions. Here are some key elements to consider when writing authentic Victorian letters:

1. Salutation:

Begin the letter with a proper salutation, addressing the recipient by their appropriate title, such as "Dear Mr.," "My Dearest," or "Honorable Madam."

2. Address and Date:

Include the sender's address and the date at the top right corner of the letter. The date format should follow the Victorian convention, typically written as "Day, Month, Year."

3. Opening:

Start the body of the letter with a polite greeting or inquiry about the recipient's well-being. Victorian letters often used phrases such as "I trust this letter finds you in good health" or "I hope this missive reaches you in high spirits."

4. Body:

The body of the letter should be the main content and can vary depending on the purpose of the correspondence. Whether it's a declaration of love, a secret message, or a plea for help, use language that reflects the character's emotions and the formality of the era. Victorian letters often included flowery language, intricate descriptions, and a formal tone.

5. Closing:

End the letter with a suitable closing phrase, such as "Yours sincerely," "With deepest regards," or "Ever faithfully." Sign the letter with the appropriate name or initials of the sender.

6. Addendums and Postscripts:

Victorian letters often included addendums or postscripts at the end for additional information or personal messages. These were enclosed within parentheses or marked with "P.S." and typically provided insights or secret disclosures.

7. Language and Style:

When writing Victorian letters, use a formal and polite tone. Incorporate intricate language, literary references, and metaphors to add depth and character to the correspondence. Capture the nuances of Victorian language and etiquette to create an authentic and immersive experience for your readers.

8. Handwriting:

Consider the handwriting styles that were common during the Victorian era. Depending on the character and their background, the handwriting can be neat and elegant or express a sense of urgency and passion. The handwriting can provide insights into the character's personality and emotions.

Examples and Inspiration

To gain inspiration and a better understanding of Victorian letters, study authentic letters written during the era. Famous writers and historical figures, such as Jane Austen and Queen Victoria, often left behind a collection of letters that provide a glimpse into the language and style of the time. These letters can serve as valuable references and sources of inspiration for writing your own Victorian correspondence.

Using Victorian Letters in your Mystical Romance Novel

Victorian letters can serve various purposes in your mystical romance novel. They can be used to convey love and passion, reveal secrets and hidden motivations, create conflict and misunderstandings, or deepen the emotional connection between characters. By incorporating authentic Victorian letters, you can enhance the authenticity and immerse readers in the romantic world of your novel.

Conclusion

Writing authentic Victorian letters and correspondence is crucial for capturing the essence of the era in your mystical romance novel. By following the structure, language, and conventions of Victorian letters, you can create a realistic and immersive experience for your readers. Use these letters to convey emotions, reveal secrets, and deepen the connections between your characters. The authenticity of Victorian correspondence will enhance the overall enchantment and charm of your mystical romance novel.

Chapter 14: Secrets and Forbidden Love: Creating Tension and Conflict

In a Victorian mystical romance novel, secrets and forbidden love can be powerful sources of tension and conflict. The allure of forbidden love and the consequences of concealed secrets can captivate readers and keep them eagerly turning the pages. This chapter will explore techniques for crafting compelling tension and conflict through secrets and forbidden love in your Victorian romance novel.

1. The Power of Secrets

Secrets have always held a certain fascination for readers, and in a Victorian mystical romance novel, they can serve as a catalyst for dramatic events and emotional turmoil. Here are some tips on incorporating secrets into your story:

1.1. Uncover secrets gradually

Reveal secrets slowly, allowing readers to unravel them alongside your characters. Succinctly hint at hidden pasts, clandestine affairs, or undisclosed identities, building tension and maintaining suspense.

1.2. Use secrets to deepen character motivations

Use secrets to shape your characters' desires, fears, and actions. The weight of a concealed truth can add complexity and depth to their personalities. Explore how secrets can guide their choices and influence their relationships.

1.3. Show the impact of revealed secrets

When a secret is finally unveiled, explore the consequences it has on your characters and their relationships. Show how trust is fractured, alliances shift, and emotions are tested. Conflict arises as characters grapple with the revelation and its aftermath.

2. Forbidden Love

Forbidden love is a staple of romantic literature, and it can be particularly enticing in a Victorian era setting, where societal norms and expectations placed restrictions on relationships. Here are some ways to create tension and conflict through forbidden love:

2.1. Establish societal expectations and constraints

Illustrate the rigid social hierarchy and moral codes of the Victorian era, which discourage relationships deemed inappropriate or scandalous. Highlight the consequences of crossing these boundaries, such as social ostracism or reputational ruin.

2.2. Create star-crossed lovers

Craft a powerful and forbidden romance between characters from different classes, social backgrounds, or even mystical realms. Exploit the tension and longing that arises from their forbidden attraction, emphasizing the obstacles they must overcome to be together.

2.3. Develop internal conflicts

Explore the internal struggles that accompany forbidden love. Delve into the conflicting emotions your characters experience as they battle their desires and wrestle with the moral implications of their feelings.

2.4. Confront external conflicts

Introduce external obstacles that stand in the way of the lovers' happiness. These could include disapproving family members, societal pressures, or rival suitors. These conflicts heighten the tension and keep readers rooting for the star-crossed couple.

3. Balancing Secrets and Forbidden Love

When secrets and forbidden love intertwine, they create a potent combination that propels the narrative forward. Here are some tips for effectively balancing these elements:

3.1. Use secrets to heighten the forbidden love

Unveil secrets that deepen the forbidden love, adding complexity to the relationship and intensifying the stakes. The revelation of a hidden past or an unexpected connection can further complicate the lovers' journey.

3.2. Explore the consequences of hidden love

Portray the ramifications of the forbidden love and the choices characters must make. Highlight the sacrifices, internal conflicts, and external obstacles they face in order to pursue their feelings.

3.3. Write moments of emotional conflict

Craft powerful scenes where characters' emotions are at odds with societal expectations or their own sense of duty. Show the internal turmoil as they grapple with their love and the desire to maintain appearances or conform to societal norms.

3.4. Use secrets to drive the plot

Integrate secrets into the plot to create twists and turns that escalate tension. The revelation of a hidden secret can act as a catalyst for conflicts, leading to confrontations, betrayals, or unexpected alliances. Incorporating secrets and forbidden love into your Victorian mystical romance novel will captivate readers and keep them engaged in the characters' journeys. By gradually revealing secrets, exploring the emotional consequences, and crafting powerful forbidden love stories, you can create compelling tension and conflict that will leave readers eagerly turning the pages. Next chapter: Chapter 15: Balancing Romance and Mystery

Chapter 15: Balancing Romance and Mystery

In a Victorian mystical romance novel, striking a balance between romance and mystery is essential for creating a captivating and engaging story. Both elements play significant roles in keeping readers enthralled, as they yearn for both love and intrigue. This chapter will explore effective techniques for balancing romance and mystery in your writing, ensuring that both aspects are thoughtfully incorporated to enhance the overall reading experience.

Understanding the Importance of Balancing Romance and Mystery

Balancing romance and mystery is crucial to creating a well-rounded narrative that appeals to readers of both genres. By intertwining these elements, you can create a story that evokes both emotional connection and thrilling suspense. The romance adds depth and attachment to the characters, while the mystery keeps readers on the edge of their seats, eager to unravel secrets and discover hidden truths. When done skillfully, the combination of romance and mystery enhances the overall impact of the story, leaving a lasting impression on readers.

Building Emotional Connections

Romance is a vital aspect of any Victorian mystical romance novel. It is essential to invest time and effort in developing the emotional connection between your characters. Readers should feel the chemistry and intensity between the protagonists, allowing them to become emotionally invested in their relationship. Showcasing genuine moments of tenderness, vulnerability, and passion will help readers to root for the couple and become engrossed in their love story.

Techniques for Balancing Romance and Mystery

1. **Showcase Smoldering Tension:** Create an air of intrigue and mystery within the romantic interactions between the main characters. Foreshadowing and subtle hints can keep readers guessing about hidden motives or secrets, maintaining an element of suspense alongside the growing love between the protagonists. 2. **Intertwine Romantic Moments with Clues:** Use pivotal romantic scenes as opportunities to drop subtle hints or clues that advance the mystery plot. This allows you to maintain a sense of progression in both the romance and the mystery, keeping readers engaged on multiple fronts. 3. **Use Conflict to Fuel Both Elements:** Conflict is a powerful tool that can serve both the romance and mystery aspects of your novel. Develop conflicts that arise from both romantic and mysterious circumstances, as this will create tension and heighten the stakes for your characters. 4. **Create Dual Pacing:** Alternating between slower, more introspective moments of romance and fast-paced, tension-filled moments of mystery can create a balanced and dynamic pace for your story. This keeps readers engaged as they navigate through the highs and lows of both genres. 5. **Reveal Secrets at the Right Time:** Timely revelation of mysteries and secrets is crucial. Share important information with readers in a way that builds anticipation and adds depth to both the romantic and mysterious plotlines without overwhelming or confusing them.

Embracing the Unexpected

One of the joys of writing a Victorian mystical romance novel is the opportunity to surprise and delight readers with unexpected twists and turns. Balancing romance and mystery allows for the unexpected to flourish, creating unforgettable moments that will keep readers hooked until the very end. Whether it's a shocking revelation, an unexpected connection between characters, or an unforeseen outcome, embracing the unexpected adds an element of intrigue that elevates the overall reading experience.

Conclusion

In a Victorian mystical romance novel, balancing romance and mystery is key to creating a compelling and immersive story. By carefully merging these elements, you can engage readers on multiple fronts, filling their hearts with emotions and minds with suspense. Remember to build emotional connections, intertwine romantic moments with clues, use conflict effectively, employ dual pacing, and embrace the unexpected. In doing so, you will create a harmonious blend of romance and mystery that will captivate and enthrall readers from beginning to end.

Chapter 16: Weaving Historical Events into Your Story

Historical events can add depth and authenticity to a Victorian mystical romance novel. By incorporating real-life events into your story, you can transport readers back in time and immerse them in the rich tapestry of the Victorian era. Here are some tips for effectively weaving historical events into your narrative:

Researching Historical Events

Before you can incorporate historical events into your story, it's crucial to conduct thorough research. Dive into the annals of history to uncover significant events that occurred during the Victorian era. Consult historical records, books, newspapers, and online resources to gain a comprehensive understanding of the events you plan to include. Focus on events that align with the themes of your novel and have the potential to enhance your mystical romance storyline. For example, if your novel revolves around supernatural occurrences, look for historical events that involve spiritualism, seances, or paranormal phenomena.

Choosing the Right Events

Once you have a solid understanding of the historical events during the Victorian era, carefully select the ones that will complement your storyline. Consider events that provide opportunities for conflict, intrigue, or romance. Look for events that can act as catalysts for character development or plot twists. For example, if your protagonist is a young woman seeking independence, you could incorporate the women's suffrage movement into your story. This historical event could serve as a backdrop for the protagonist's journey towards self-discovery and empowerment.

Integrating Events Seamlessly

To effectively weave historical events into your story, it's important to integrate them seamlessly with the narrative. Avoid inserting historical events as mere exposition or information dumps. Instead, find creative ways to incorporate them into the plot, dialogue, or character arcs. One approach is to use historical events as a backdrop or catalyst for the actions and decisions of your characters. For instance, if your story takes place during the Great Exhibition of 1851, you could have your characters attend the exhibition and use it as a setting for a pivotal scene or interaction. Another way to integrate historical events is through the reactions and emotions of your characters. Show how the events impact their lives, beliefs, or relationships. This will make the events feel more organic and relatable to readers.

Accuracy and Authenticity

While incorporating historical events, it is crucial to maintain accuracy and authenticity. Ensure that the events you include align with the historical timeline and societal norms of the Victorian era. Pay attention to details, such as dates, locations, and the cultural context surrounding the events. Use primary and secondary sources for reference to ensure your portrayal of the events is accurate. If necessary, consult experts or historians to validate the historical accuracy of your narrative.

Adding Drama and Depth

When incorporating historical events, use them to add drama and depth to your story. Historical events can create anticipation, suspense, or conflict, driving the plot forward and engaging readers. They can also provide an opportunity to explore the impact of historical events on the lives of your characters. You can highlight the contrast between the grandeur of historical events and the intimate moments between your characters. For example, juxtapose a lavish social event with a heartfelt confession of love or a secret meeting in the shadows. This contrast adds texture and emotional depth to your narrative. In conclusion, weaving historical events into your Victorian mystical romance novel can enhance its authenticity and captivate readers. Conduct thorough research, choose events that align with your story's themes, integrate them seamlessly, maintain accuracy and authenticity, and use these events to add drama and depth to your narrative. By skillfully incorporating historical events, you can transport readers to the Victorian era and create a compelling and immersive reading experience.

Chapter 17: Capturing the Victorian Society

In a Victorian mystical romance novel, it is essential to accurately depict the society of the era. Victorian society was a complex and hierarchical structure with distinct social classes and a rigid set of expectations and norms. Capturing the essence of this society will add depth and authenticity to your story.

Understanding the Social Classes

The Victorian era was marked by a strict class system that divided society into three main classes: the upper class, the middle class, and the working class. Each class had its own set of rules, values, and expectations. The upper class, often referred to as the aristocracy, consisted of the wealthiest and most influential individuals in society. They were born into nobility and inherited their status. They held tremendous power and were known for their extravagant lifestyles and grand estates. When portraying the upper class in your novel, focus on their opulent surroundings, lavish parties, and intricate social rituals. The middle class, also known as the bourgeoisie, was composed of professionals, businessmen, and successful merchants. They valued hard work, education, and respectability. The middle class sought to emulate the behaviors and values of the upper class, often aspiring to climb the social ladder. When writing about the middle class, explore their ambitions, aspirations, and struggles to maintain social standing. The working class, the largest segment of society, encompassed laborers, servants, and factory workers. They lived in poverty and faced harsh working conditions. Despite their challenging circumstances, the working class often exhibited resilience, community spirit, and a sense of camaraderie. Portraying the working class in your novel allows you to shed light on the social injustices and inequalities of the era.

Social Expectations and Manners

Victorian society had a strict code of conduct and expected individuals to adhere to specific social norms and etiquette. It is crucial to incorporate these expectations when portraying characters and their interactions. Incorporate the values of modesty, chastity, and decorum into your characters' behavior. Avoid overt displays of emotions and physical affection, as Victorian society deemed such displays inappropriate. Women were expected to be demure, submissive, and primarily devoted to their families and households. Men were to be chivalrous, responsible, and the providers for their families. Politeness and proper manners were highly valued, with emphasis placed on addressing people with respect and using formal language. Pay attention to social rituals such as calling cards, formal introductions, and proper seating arrangements. Additionally, Victorian society grappled with issues of morality and the definition of respectability. The characters in your novel can navigate these moral dilemmas and confront the expectations of society, adding depth and complexity to their stories.

Contrasting Realities

While Victorian society upheld a façade of respectability and propriety, there were also darker aspects hidden beneath the surface. Poverty, crime, and vice were prevalent in the overcrowded cities. Explore the contrast between the glittering upper-class parties and the squalor of the working-class neighborhoods. Illustrate the struggles faced by the lower classes and the societal taboos they encountered. By capturing the contradictions and complexities of Victorian society, you can create a vivid and immersive world for your readers. Showcasing the social dynamics, expectations, and contradictions will add depth and realism to your mystical romance novel set in the Victorian era. So, as you delve into your writing, pay close attention to the social classes, social expectations, and contrasting realities of Victorian society. By weaving these elements into your story, you will transport readers to a time where societal roles and expectations shaped individuals' lives, adding layers of authenticity to your mystical romance novel.

Chapter 18: Crafting Unforgettable Romantic Moments

Romantic moments are at the heart of a Victorian mystical romance novel. These moments not only deepen the connection between characters but also captivate readers and evoke a range of emotions. In this chapter, we will explore techniques for crafting unforgettable romantic moments that will leave a lasting impact on your readers.

Creating Chemistry between Characters

Chemistry between characters is essential for building romantic moments. By creating believable and compelling connections, readers will be invested in the romance and root for the characters to be together. Consider the following tips to create chemistry: 1. Establish shared interests: Find common ground between the characters, whether it's a love for literature, art, or adventure. These shared interests will create a bond between them and serve as a foundation for their romance. 2. Develop meaningful conversations: Engage the characters in deep and meaningful conversations that showcase their emotional connection. Have them discuss their hopes, dreams, and fears, allowing readers to witness their vulnerability and emotional depth. 3. Use subtle gestures and body language: Pay attention to the subtle ways characters communicate their feelings through body language and gestures. A touch, a lingering gaze, or a stolen kiss can convey a multitude of emotions without a single word spoken.

Setting the Scene

The setting plays a crucial role in crafting romantic moments. The Victorian era offers a plethora of options for creating atmospheric and intimate settings. Consider the following: 1. Candlelit dinners: Set the scene with a romantic dinner by candlelight. Describe the flickering flames, the exquisite table settings, and the tantalizing aroma of the food. This creates a sense of intimacy and sets the stage for a heartfelt conversation between the characters. 2. Moonlit strolls: Take advantage of the enchanting atmosphere of a moonlit night. Have your characters stroll hand in hand through a picturesque park or along a moonlit beach, allowing them to share intimate moments while basking in the glow of the moon. 3. Exquisite gardens: Victorian gardens were known for their beauty and serenity. Use a well-manicured garden as a backdrop for a romantic encounter. Describe the blooming flowers, the sweet fragrance in the air, and the secluded nooks where characters can steal away for whispered confessions.

Writing Heartfelt Declarations of Love

Emotions run high in a romantic moment, and heartfelt declarations of love can leave a lasting impact on readers. Here are some tips for writing memorable declarations: 1. Avoid clichés: Steer clear of overused phrases and clichés. Instead, focus on crafting unique and sincere expressions of love that reflect the characters' personalities and the depth of their emotions. 2. Be specific: When a character declares their love, be specific about what they love about the other person. Is it their laughter, kindness, or intelligence? These specific details make the declaration feel more authentic and personal. 3. Show vulnerability: Allow your characters to express their vulnerability when declaring their love. This vulnerability adds depth and makes the moment more relatable to readers.

Intensifying the Romantic Moment with Tension

Tension is a powerful tool for intensifying romantic moments. By incorporating conflict or obstacles, you can heighten the emotional impact and keep readers engrossed in the story. Consider the following techniques: 1. Internal conflicts: Explore the internal conflicts that characters face when admitting their feelings. This could include their fear of rejection, doubts about their own worthiness, or conflicts between duty and desire. 2. External conflicts: Introduce external conflicts that threaten the characters' chance at happiness. This could involve societal expectations, parental disapproval, or past traumas. These conflicts create stakes and add layers of tension to the romantic moment. 3. Cliffhangers: End a romantic moment on a cliffhanger, leaving readers wanting more. This can be done by introducing unexpected obstacles or unresolved questions, ensuring that the romantic tension carries on throughout the story. Remember, the key to crafting unforgettable romantic moments is to engage readers' emotions and create a sense of genuine connection between the characters. By using chemistry, atmospheric settings, heartfelt declarations, and tension, you can create romantic moments that will stay with readers long after they finish your Victorian mystical romance novel. Next chapter we will discuss Chapter 19: Embracing Marie Corelli's Unique Writing Style.

Chapter 19: Embracing Marie Corelli's Unique Writing Style

Marie Corelli was a prolific Victorian novelist known for her distinctive writing style and her ability to create captivating mystical romance novels. In this chapter, we will explore the key elements of Marie Corelli's writing style and how to embrace her unique approach in your own Victorian mystical romance novel.

The Themes of Love and Destiny

One of the central themes in Marie Corelli's novels is the power of love and destiny. She often intertwined these themes, portraying love as a force that transcends time and brings characters together against all odds. Embrace this theme in your writing by focusing on the profound connection between your protagonists and how their love shapes their destinies.

Mystical and Supernatural Elements

Corelli's novels often incorporated mystical and supernatural elements, adding a touch of magic to her storytelling. From visions and prophecies to encounters with otherworldly beings, these elements heightened the intrigue and wonder of her novels. To capture Corelli's unique style, consider weaving mystical and supernatural elements into your own Victorian mystical romance novel. Whether it be a mysterious talisman or a ghostly apparition, these elements can add an extra layer of enchantment to your story.

Emotional Depth and Intensity

Marie Corelli's writing was known for its emotional depth and intensity. She delved into the innermost thoughts and feelings of her characters, often describing their intense emotions with vivid imagery and poetic language. To embrace Corelli's writing style, focus on creating characters with rich inner lives and explore their emotional journeys throughout the novel. Allow the readers to experience the intensity of their emotions, from overwhelming joy to heart-wrenching despair.

Victorian Society Critiques

Corelli's novels often contained subtle critiques of Victorian society, challenging its rigid norms and values. She explored themes of social inequality, hypocrisy, and the corruption of power, often using her characters to voice these critiques. Embrace this aspect of Corelli's writing style by incorporating social commentary into your own Victorian mystical romance novel. Use your characters and their experiences to shed light on the flaws and contradictions of Victorian society.

Romantic and Sensational Language

Marie Corelli's writing style was characterized by its romantic and sensational language. She used flowery descriptions, elaborate metaphors, and passionate language to evoke strong emotions in her readers. To capture Corelli's unique style, experiment with descriptive language that paints vivid pictures in the reader's mind. Allow your characters to express their emotions in passionate and poetic ways, enhancing the intensity of their romantic moments.

Engaging Narrative and Pacing

Marie Corelli was a master of keeping her readers engaged from start to finish. Her novels were filled with gripping plotlines, unexpected twists, and cliffhangers that left readers eagerly turning the pages. Embrace Corelli's engaging narrative style by creating a plot that keeps readers on the edge of their seats. Incorporate unexpected twists and turns into your storyline, and end chapters with suspenseful moments to keep readers wanting more.

A Focus on Morality and Redemption

Corelli's novels often explored themes of morality and redemption. Characters faced moral dilemmas and had to confront their own flaws and past mistakes. Embrace Corelli's focus on morality and redemption by incorporating these elements into your own Victorian mystical romance novel. Show how your characters grapple with their own moral compass and strive for redemption, adding depth and complexity to their journeys. Incorporating Marie Corelli's unique writing style into your own Victorian mystical romance novel can elevate your storytelling and transport readers into a world of fantastical love and enchantment. Embrace the themes of love and destiny, weave in mystical and supernatural elements, dive deep into the emotional lives of your characters, critique Victorian society, use romantic and sensational language, maintain an engaging narrative and pacing, and explore the themes of morality and redemption. By embracing Corelli's style, you can create a novel that captivates readers and leaves a lasting impression.

Chapter 20: Researching Medical and Scientific Advancements in the Victorian Era

The Victorian era was a period of significant advancements in medicine and science. In this chapter, we will explore the key developments in medical and scientific knowledge during this time, and how to accurately incorporate them into your Victorian mystical romance novel.

1. The Progress of Medicine

During the Victorian era, medicine made remarkable strides, thanks to advances in scientific knowledge and technological innovations. Here are some important areas to research:

1.1 Surgical Techniques

Research the evolving surgical techniques and procedures of the era. Develop an understanding of the tools and equipment used, such as scalpels, forceps, and ligatures. Familiarize yourself with notable surgeons and their contributions, like James Syme and Joseph Lister. Integrate these details into your novel to bring authenticity to any medical scenes or characters.

1.2 Anesthesia and Pain Relief

Anesthesia was another significant breakthrough during the Victorian era. Chloroform and ether were widely used to numb pain during surgical procedures. Study the administration and effects of anesthesia, and consider incorporating these elements into your novel when writing medical scenes or procedures.

1.3 Medical Training and Education

Research the process and requirements for medical training during the Victorian era. Understand the different levels of medical professionals, such as surgeons, physicians, and nurses. Explore the educational institutions and the courses they offered. This knowledge will help you create believable medical characters and their backgrounds.

2. Scientific Advancements

Apart from medical advancements, the Victorian era also witnessed significant progress in various scientific fields. Here are some areas to explore:

2.1 Darwin's Theory of Evolution

Charles Darwin's theory of evolution, published in 1859, had a profound impact on Victorian society. Familiarize yourself with the key concepts of Darwinism and the debates it sparked during the era. Consider incorporating elements of this scientific theory into your novel, either as a catalyst for conflict or as a backdrop for discussion among characters.

2.2 Advances in Chemistry

Research the discoveries and breakthroughs in the field of chemistry during the Victorian era. Explore key figures such as Michael Faraday and Dmitri Mendeleev. Understand the Victorian understanding of chemicals and their effects, as well as the development of laboratory equipment. This knowledge will enable you to create scientifically accurate scenes or in-depth discussions among characters.

2.3 Technological Innovation

The Victorian era witnessed remarkable advancements in technology, such as the telegraph, steam engines, and photography. Research these innovations and consider integrating them into your story. Show how these technological advancements shape various aspects of Victorian society, from communication to transportation and even scientific experiments.

3. Ethical Considerations

While researching medical and scientific advancements, it is essential to consider the ethical dilemmas and controversies surrounding these developments. Addressing these topics in your novel can add depth and complexity to your characters and their moral choices.

3.1 Medical Ethics

Explore the ethical debates surrounding medical practices during the Victorian era. Delve into issues such as medical experimentation, patient consent, and the balance between scientific progress and patient welfare. Incorporate these ethical considerations into the decisions and actions of your medical characters.

3.2 Scientific Responsibility

Consider the responsibilities scientists and researchers had during the Victorian era. Research the potential consequences of their discoveries and how they grappled with the ethical implications of their work. Use these ethical dilemmas as fuel for conflict or character growth in your mystical romance novel.

4. Authenticity in Writing

When incorporating medical and scientific advancements into your Victorian mystical romance novel, it is crucial to prioritize historical accuracy. While some creative liberties may be taken, strive to maintain authenticity in your depictions of the era's medical and scientific knowledge.

4.1 Thorough Research

Thoroughly research medical practices, scientific theories, and technological innovations of the Victorian era. Utilize reputable sources such as historical texts, journals, and academic articles. This attention to detail will allow you to create a rich and believable world for your readers.

4.2 Seamlessly Integrate Knowledge

Integrate your research seamlessly into your narrative, avoiding information dumps or overwhelming the reader. Use details sparingly and purposefully, ensuring they enhance the story and immerse readers in the Victorian era.

4.3 Consulting Experts

If possible, consult with experts or professionals in the fields of medicine and science. Their insights and guidance will provide valuable and accurate information to enhance the authenticity of your novel. Researching medical and scientific advancements in the Victorian era will add depth, realism, and historical accuracy to your mystical romance novel. By incorporating these elements thoughtfully, you can create a captivating story that transports readers to a world where love, magic, and progress intertwine in the enigmatic Victorian era.

Chapter 21: Exploring Victorian Superstitions and Beliefs

Victorian England was a time of great fascination with the supernatural and mystical beliefs. It was an era where superstitions held a powerful influence on people's lives. Exploring Victorian superstitions and beliefs can add depth and authenticity to your mystical romance novel set in this time period. In this chapter, we will delve into some of the most prevalent Victorian superstitions and beliefs, providing you with insight into the mindset of the era.

The Power of Superstitions

Superstitions were deeply ingrained in Victorian society, shaping the way people lived and interacted with the world around them. These beliefs were often rooted in religion, folklore, and ancient customs. Understanding the power of superstitions is essential for creating an immersive and authentic world in your novel.

Common Superstitions

One of the most pervasive superstitions of the Victorian era was the belief in omens and signs. People would look for symbols and occurrences that foretold good or bad luck. For example, a black cat crossing one's path was seen as a sign of impending misfortune, while finding a four-leaf clover was believed to bring good luck. Victorians also had strong beliefs about numbers. The number 13, for instance, was considered unlucky and was often avoided at all costs. Friday the 13th was regarded as an especially ominous day. Conversely, the number 7 was seen as lucky, and many rituals and customs were built around it. Old wives' tales were also prevalent in Victorian society. These were myths and sayings passed down through generations, often providing guidance or cautionary advice. For example, it was said that if you broke a mirror, you would have seven years of bad luck. Touching wood or knocking on wood to ward off misfortune was another common practice.

Beliefs in the Supernatural

Victorians held a strong belief in the existence of ghosts, spirits, and other supernatural beings. The spiritualist movement gained popularity during this time, with seances and mediumship becoming common practices. Spiritualists claimed to communicate with the dead and provide messages from beyond the grave. Another supernatural belief was in the power of charms and talismans. People carried amulets, such as lucky coins or rabbit's feet, to protect themselves from harm and bring good fortune. The use of charms and talismans can add an intriguing and mystical element to your novel.

Taboos and Superstitions Surrounding Love and Marriage

Love and marriage held a central place in Victorian society, and there were numerous superstitions and taboos surrounding these topics. For instance, it was considered unlucky to see the bride in her wedding dress before the ceremony. Additionally, it was believed that wearing opals as bridal jewelry brought bad luck. There were also superstitions related to courtship. For example, giving a loved one a hawthorn blossom was seen as a declaration of imminent marriage. It was believed that if a woman placed a rosemary sprig under her pillow, she would dream of her future husband.

Incorporating Superstitions into Your Novel

To incorporate Victorian superstitions and beliefs into your mystical romance novel, consider how they can influence your characters' actions, beliefs, and relationships. You can use superstitions to create tension and conflict, or to enhance the mystique and atmosphere of your story. Think about how your characters might react to superstitions. Do they dismiss them as mere nonsense, or do they live their lives strictly adhering to these beliefs? How might these superstitions impact their decisions and interactions with others? Furthermore, you can use superstitions as plot devices. Perhaps a character's belief in an omen leads them down a certain path, or a forbidden love affair is deemed doomed due to a particular superstition. Superstitions can add depth and complexity to your storyline, creating a rich and immersive reading experience. Remember to conduct thorough research to ensure accuracy when incorporating Victorian superstitions and beliefs into your novel. This will allow you to create an authentic portrayal of the era's mindset and enhance the mystical elements of your story. In the next chapter, we will explore Victorian social etiquette and manners, providing you with insights on how to accurately depict the intricate codes of behavior that governed Victorian society.

Chapter 22: Victorian Social Etiquette and Manners

Victorian society was known for its strict social norms and expectations, particularly when it came to etiquette and manners. Understanding these customs is essential for creating an authentic and immersive world in a mystical romance novel set in the Victorian era. In this chapter, we will explore the various aspects of Victorian social etiquette and manners that can add depth and realism to your story.

Politeness and Decorum

Politeness and decorum were highly valued in Victorian society. People were expected to conduct themselves with grace and poise, regardless of their social class. Good manners were seen as a reflection of moral character and respectability. It was customary for individuals to greet each other politely, with a firm handshake or a respectful nod of the head. Men were expected to hold doors open for women and allow them to enter rooms first. When seated at a dining table, it was polite to wait for everyone to be served before beginning to eat.

Modesty and Demureness

Victorian society had strict expectations for women, who were expected to be modest and demure. They were encouraged to dress and behave in a way that would not attract too much attention or cause scandal. Women were expected to speak softly and avoid engaging in debates or discussions that were considered inappropriate for their gender. Men, on the other hand, were expected to be chivalrous and responsible. They were supposed to protect and provide for their families, as well as demonstrate good manners and proper behavior.

Physical Contact and Dancing

Physical contact was limited in Victorian society, especially between men and women who were not married or closely related. Holding hands or public displays of affection were generally frowned upon. Even married couples were expected to maintain a certain level of modesty in public. However, dancing provided a socially acceptable way for individuals to interact and engage in physical contact. The waltz was a popular dance during the Victorian era, characterized by graceful movements and close proximity. Other formal dances, such as the quadrille and the polka, also allowed for controlled physical contact.

Conversation and Topics of Discussion

Light-hearted and pleasant conversations were the norm in Victorian society. Subjects that were considered taboo, such as politics and religion, were generally avoided in polite company. Instead, topics such as fashion, literature, and current events were more commonly discussed. Victorian society placed a strong emphasis on the art of conversation, praising those who were eloquent and well-spoken. It was important to speak clearly and enunciate words properly. Interrupting or speaking too loudly was seen as disrespectful.

Social Hierarchy and Formalities

Victorian society had a distinct social hierarchy, with the upper class at the top, followed by the middle class and the working class. Respect and deference were expected towards those of higher social status. When addressing someone of higher social standing, it was customary to use honorific titles, such as "Sir" or "Madam." In formal settings, individuals were expected to curtsy or bow as a sign of respect.

Dining Etiquette

Dining etiquette was of utmost importance in Victorian society, especially for those in the upper classes. Proper table manners and a knowledge of dining etiquette were essential. Napkins were to be placed on one's lap, elbows were to be kept off the table, and cutlery was to be used appropriately. To indicate that one had finished eating, the knife and fork were placed together on the plate, with the handles facing towards the right.

Conclusion

Understanding Victorian social etiquette and manners is crucial for creating an authentic and immersive world in a mystical romance novel set in the Victorian era. Politeness, decorum, modesty, limited physical contact, refined conversation topics, and respect for social hierarchy were all important aspects of Victorian society. Incorporating these customs into your writing will add depth and realism to your story, allowing readers to truly immerse themselves in the magical world of the Victorian era.

Chapter 23: Writing a Heartwarming Victorian Christmas Tale

In the Victorian era, Christmas was a cherished holiday filled with traditions and festivities. It was a time when families came together, and communities celebrated the spirit of goodwill and joy. Writing a heartwarming Victorian Christmas tale allows you to capture the essence of this magical time and create a story that will touch the hearts of your readers.

1. Setting the Scene

To create a heartwarming Victorian Christmas tale, it is essential to evoke a sense of nostalgia and create a vivid setting. Begin by describing the wintry landscape with snow-covered streets, decorated town squares, and Christmas markets filled with laughter and music. Incorporate the sound of carolers singing familiar hymns and the smell of roasted chestnuts. Show the contrast between the cozy warmth inside homes and the crisp winter air outside. Paint a picture that transports your readers to the enchanting world of Victorian Christmas.

2. Embracing Traditions

Victorian Christmas traditions played a significant role in shaping the holiday season. Incorporate these traditions into your story to create a sense of authenticity and nostalgia. Include the decoration of the Christmas tree with candles, ornaments, and garlands. Describe the gathering of family and friends around the tree, exchanging gifts and stories. Capture the anticipation of hanging stockings by the fireplace, waiting for Santa Claus to arrive. Show the joy of preparing a grand feast with roast turkey, plum pudding, and mince pies. By embracing these traditions, you will immerse your readers in the magic of a Victorian Christmas.

3. Characters and Relationships

In a heartwarming Victorian Christmas tale, focus on creating relatable and endearing characters. Develop strong family bonds and cherished friendships. Show the love, compassion, and generosity that define the holiday season. Include characters from different walks of life, providing opportunities for unlikely friendships and acts of kindness. Explore the themes of forgiveness, redemption, and the power of second chances. By emphasizing the importance of relationships, you will resonate with readers and evoke the true spirit of Christmas.

4. Themes of Love and Giving

Christmas is a time for love and giving. Explore these themes in your Victorian Christmas tale to create a heartwarming narrative. Show acts of selflessness and kindness as characters reach out to those in need. Include charitable endeavors such as organizing a Christmas fundraiser or providing a warm meal for the less fortunate. Explore the transformative power of love and forgiveness, allowing your characters to experience personal growth and redemption. By highlighting these themes, you will create a story that warms the hearts of your readers.

5. Capturing the Magic

Victorian Christmas tales often incorporate a touch of magic. Whether it be a nostalgic moment, a spark of hope, or a small miracle, these magical elements enhance the heartwarming nature of your story. Consider including moments of serendipity, coincidence, or unexpected reunions. Emphasize the power of faith and belief in miracles. Allow your characters to experience something extraordinary that embodies the enchantment of the season. By capturing the magic, you will transport your readers into a world where anything is possible.

6. A Touch of Romance

Romance can add an extra layer of warmth and emotion to your Victorian Christmas tale. It can be a blossoming love story or a rekindled flame between characters. Show the power of love during the holiday season, where hearts are open and emotions are heightened. Create tender moments, stolen glances, and unforgettable declarations of love that will make your readers swoon. Keep the romance heartwarming and subtle, allowing it to complement the overall theme of your Christmas tale. In writing a heartwarming Victorian Christmas tale, remember to infuse your story with nostalgia, love, kindness, and the magic of the holiday season. Create relatable characters, embrace traditions, and evoke a sense of joy and generosity. By capturing the spirit of a Victorian Christmas, you will create a story that resonates with readers and leaves them with a warm and glowing heart. Stay tuned for Chapter 24: Handling Sensitivity and Controversial Topics.

Chapter 24: Handling Sensitivity and Controversial Topics

In writing a Victorian mystical romance novel, it is important to handle sensitivity and controversial topics with care and respect. The Victorian era was a time of strict social norms and moral righteousness, which can pose challenges when addressing sensitive subjects. However, addressing these topics in a thoughtful and nuanced way can add depth to your story and enhance the overall reading experience. When approaching sensitive topics, it is crucial to conduct thorough research and understand the historical context surrounding them. This will ensure that your portrayal is accurate and authentic. Take the time to explore different perspectives and viewpoints, as this will help you create well-rounded and multi-dimensional characters. Consider the societal norms, values, and beliefs of the Victorian era, and how these may influence the way your characters navigate these sensitive topics. One key aspect of handling sensitivity and controversial topics is to give a voice to marginalized groups. Victorian society had its share of inequality and discrimination, and it is important to acknowledge and address these issues in your novel. By giving voice to underrepresented characters and shedding light on their experiences, you can create a more inclusive and empathetic story. Additionally, it is important to be mindful of the impact your words may have on readers. Take the time to consider the potential emotional impact of addressing sensitive subjects and controversial topics. Be aware of the potential triggers and sensitivities that your readers may have and handle these subjects with sensitivity and care. In handling controversial topics, it is important to strike a balance between historical accuracy and modern sensibilities. While it is crucial to accurately portray the mindset and values of the Victorian era, it is equally important to approach these topics through a contemporary lens. This means challenging and critiquing the social norms and prejudices of the time, while also promoting understanding and empathy. Remember that sensitivity readers can be valuable resources in this process. These individuals can provide insights and perspectives that may help you avoid misrepresentations and stereotypes. Their feedback can help ensure that you handle sensitive topics respectfully and responsibly. In conclusion, handling sensitivity and controversial topics in a Victorian mystical romance novel requires thoughtful consideration and research. By approaching these subjects with care, empathy, and understanding, you can create a story that is both engaging and respectful. Always strive for authenticity, accuracy, and inclusivity in your portrayal of sensitive subjects, and be open to feedback and guidance from sensitivity readers.

Chapter 25: Injecting Humor into Your Mystical Romance Novel

Injecting humor into a Victorian mystical romance novel can add a delightful touch and provide a balance to the more serious and supernatural elements of the story. Humor not only entertains readers but also helps to create memorable and relatable characters. Incorporating humor allows readers to connect with the story on a deeper level and creates a more immersive and enjoyable reading experience. Here are some tips on how to effectively inject humor into your mystical romance novel:

1. Develop quirky and comedic characters

One way to introduce humor is by creating characters with amusing and eccentric traits. Think of a character who is perpetually clumsy or has a unique way of viewing the world. Their amusing antics and humorous dialogue can bring a light-hearted element to the story and provide comedic relief. Just ensure that the humor aligns with the overall tone of the novel and doesn't detract from the romantic and mystical aspects.

2. Use situational humor

Leveraging situational humor can add comedic moments to your story. Consider placing your characters in humorous or absurd situations that bring out their comedic reactions. For example, a character could stumble upon a secret magical artifact and accidentally activate it, leading to unintended and humorous consequences. These unexpected situations can provide opportunities for witty banter and comedic misunderstandings.

3. Incorporate humorous dialogue

Crafting witty and clever dialogue is an effective way to infuse humor into your novel. Develop characters with a sharp sense of humor and have them engage in playful banter or exchange humorous remarks. Use comedic timing and comedic devices such as wordplay, puns, and sarcasm to create humorous exchanges between characters. Dialogue can be a powerful tool for injecting humor while also revealing character traits and building relationships.

4. Employ comedic foils and sidekicks

Introducing humorous foils or sidekick characters can enhance the comedic elements of your novel. These characters can provide comic relief through their contrasting personalities or by acting as comedic buffers in tense or dramatic situations. Foils and sidekicks are often the source of humorous interactions and can lighten the overall mood of the story.

5. Utilize comedic descriptions and metaphors

Infusing your narration with comedic descriptions and metaphors can enhance the humor in your novel. Consider using exaggerated or unexpected comparisons to create comedic effect. Play with language and use imagery that brings a smile to the reader's face. These humorous descriptions can provide a fresh perspective and keep readers engaged.

6. Balance humor with the overall tone

While humor can enliven the story, it's important to strike a balance that aligns with the overall tone of your mystical romance novel. Ensure that the humor doesn't overshadow the emotional depth, romance, and supernatural elements. Humor should complement and enhance the story, rather than detract from its underlying themes. Injecting humor into your Victorian mystical romance novel can make it a delightfully entertaining experience for readers. It allows readers to connect with the characters, brings lightness to the story, and adds depth to their emotional journey. By incorporating these tips, you can infuse humor seamlessly and enhance the overall reading experience of your novel.

Chapter 26: The Role of Nature in Your Writing

Nature plays a significant role in Victorian mystical romance novels, as it not only serves as a backdrop for the story but also becomes a character in itself. The lush landscapes and the beauty of the natural world can enhance the atmosphere, deepen emotions, and provide metaphors and symbolism for themes and character development.

Connecting Characters with Nature

Incorporating nature into your writing allows you to create a deeper connection between your characters and their environment. Showcasing how they interact with nature can reveal their personalities and emotions. For example, a heroine who finds solace in long walks through the woods may be seen as independent and introspective. A hero who tends to a garden might represent nurturing and sensitivity. Consider the following ways to connect your characters with nature: - Scenic descriptions: Use detailed descriptions of landscapes, gardens, or weather, and observe how your characters react to their surroundings. Does the sight of a breathtaking sunset bring forth feelings of awe and wonder or ignite a sense of melancholy? - Sensory experiences: Include sensory details to immerse your readers in the natural world. Describe the scent of flowers, the feel of grass underfoot, or the sound of birds singing. These details can evoke emotions and create a vivid reading experience. - Nature as a metaphor: Use nature as a metaphor to enhance your storytelling. A blooming garden can represent hope and growth, while a stormy sky may foreshadow turmoil and conflict. Consider how these natural elements can mirror the emotional journey of your characters.

Symbolism and Imagery in Nature

Nature provides abundant opportunities for symbolism and imagery in Victorian mystical romance novels. By infusing elements of the natural world into your story, you can deepen its themes and add layers of meaning. Consider the following examples: - Seasons: Each season brings its own symbolism and can reflect the emotional and narrative arc of your story. Spring symbolizes renewal and new beginnings, while autumn represents transition and change. Use descriptions of nature's cycles to mirror the growth and transformation of your characters. - Flowers and plants: Flowers and plants have symbolic meanings attached to them. Roses often symbolize love and passion, while lilies can represent purity and innocence. Incorporate these symbols into your narrative to enhance the emotional depth of your story. - Animals and creatures: Animals can act as motifs in your novel, representing certain traits or foreshadowing events. For instance, a black cat can symbolize mystery and magic, while a butterfly can embody transformation and rebirth.

Using Nature to Create Atmosphere and Mood

Nature has the power to create atmosphere and set the mood in your Victorian mystical romance novel. By describing the natural world in a way that complements your storyline, you can transport readers into the magical setting of your story. Consider the following techniques: - Seasons and weather: Use the changing seasons and weather to shape the mood of your scenes. A bright sunny day can create a sense of joy and optimism, while a stormy night can evoke tension and mystery. - Descriptive language: Use rich and detailed descriptions to bring nature to life in your writing. Paint vivid pictures with your words by utilizing sensory details, such as the scent of wildflowers or the sound of leaves rustling in the wind. - Contrast: Create contrast between the natural world and the human world to heighten the impact of certain scenes. For example, a peaceful garden setting can provide a stark contrast to a tense conversation between characters. - Foreshadowing: Nature can be a powerful tool for foreshadowing events in your story. Use subtle cues in the natural world to hint at future plot developments or to create an air of anticipation.

Embracing the Power of Nature in Your Writing

Incorporating nature into your Victorian mystical romance novel adds depth, symbolism, and atmosphere to your storytelling. By connecting your characters with nature, using symbolism and imagery, and creating the right atmosphere and mood, you can create a truly immersive reading experience. Remember to conduct thorough research on Victorian attitudes towards nature and the natural world to ensure historical accuracy in your writing. By skillfully integrating nature into your novel, you can create a captivating and enchanting story that transports readers to the mystical realms of the Victorian era.

Chapter 27: Incorporating Historical Research Seamlessly

In any Victorian mystical romance novel, incorporating historical research seamlessly is crucial for creating an authentic and immersive reading experience. By grounding your story in historical accuracy, you can transport readers back in time to the enchanting world of the Victorian era. Here are some tips to help you seamlessly integrate your historical research into your novel:

1. Thoroughly Research the Victorian Era:

Before you even start writing, it's essential to conduct thorough research on the Victorian era. Familiarize yourself with major historical events, social norms, cultural traditions, and daily life of the time period. This will provide a solid foundation for your storytelling and help you avoid anachronisms.

2. Know Your Sources:

When researching the Victorian era, it's crucial to consult reliable sources such as academic articles, books, primary sources, and reputable websites. Be discerning and cross-reference information to ensure accuracy. Always double check dates, names, and historical details to maintain the fidelity of your novel.

3. Integrate Historical Details Organically:

Once you have gathered your research, the key is to integrate historical details into your novel organically. Avoid info-dumping or inserting historical facts in long exposition passages. Instead, sprinkle historical details throughout your narrative, weaving them into the fabric of your story. For example, rather than simply stating that your protagonist lives in a grand Victorian mansion, describe the lavish decoration of the parlor or the elegant attire worn by guests at a soirée. By immersing readers in vivid descriptions, you will transport them to the world of the Victorian era.

4. Blend Historical Figures with Fictional Characters:

Incorporating real historical figures can add depth and authenticity to your story. However, it's important to tread carefully, as historical figures should not overshadow your main characters. Use historical figures sparingly and ensure their roles are integral to the plot. Create a believable interaction between your fictional characters and historical figures, while respecting their known attributes and actions.

5. Show, Don't Tell:

Rather than providing historical information through exposition, show them through character actions, dialogue, and immersive descriptions. For example, instead of stating that your character is visiting the Great Exhibition of 1851, describe the bustling crowd, the awe-inspiring Crystal Palace, and the character's fascination with the innovative inventions on display.

6. Create an Atmosphere of Authenticity:

To create an atmosphere of authenticity, pay attention to the smaller details. Research the language, slang, and idioms of the era and incorporate them subtly into your characters' dialogue. Describe the smells, sounds, and tastes of Victorian life to transport readers into the sensory experience of the time.

7. Balance Historical Accuracy with Storytelling:

While historical accuracy is important, remember that you are writing a work of fiction. Strike a balance between staying true to the historical context and crafting an engaging and compelling story. Don't let historical details overwhelm or burden your narrative; let them enhance and enrich your storytelling.

Conclusion:

Incorporating historical research seamlessly into your Victorian mystical romance novel is a delicate and essential task. Thoroughly research the era, know your sources, and integrate historical details organically. Blend historical figures with fictional characters, show rather than tell, and create an atmosphere of authenticity. Finally, strike a balance between historical accuracy and storytelling. By following these tips, you can create a captivating and immersive reading experience that transports readers back in time to the enchanting world of the Victorian era.

Chapter 28: Creating Unforgettable Villains

In any good mystical romance novel, the hero and heroine may be the stars of the story, but it is the villain who adds the necessary conflict and tension. The villain is the catalyst for the hero and heroine's growth, the one who stands in their way, and ultimately presents the greatest challenge they must overcome. It is crucial to create a compelling and memorable antagonist that readers will love to hate.

The Role of the Villain

The villain serves a vital role in a Victorian mystical romance novel. They are the embodiment of evil, representing the dark forces that threaten the happiness and well-being of the hero and heroine. They can take many forms, from a charming sociopath to a malevolent supernatural being. The villain's actions and motivations create conflict and obstacles for the protagonists, and their presence heightens the suspense and intrigue of the story.

Characteristics of an Unforgettable Villain

To create an unforgettable villain, consider the following characteristics: 1. **Complexity:** Portray your villain as a multidimensional character with their own beliefs, desires, and motivations. They should be more than just a one-dimensional "bad guy." Give them a compelling backstory and explore their vulnerabilities, which can make them both intriguing and relatable. 2. **Motivation:** Determine what drives your villain. Are they seeking power, revenge, or simply chaos? The clearer their motivations, the more depth they will have. Their motivations should be believable and provide a strong foundation for their actions. 3. **Moral ambiguity:**

Consider giving your villain shades of gray. They don't have to be completely evil or irredeemable. Adding complexity to their moral compass can create tension and make them more compelling. 4. **Charisma:** A charismatic villain can be just as captivating as the hero or heroine. They may possess an irresistible charm or an ability to manipulate others. Use their charisma to draw both characters and readers in, making them question their loyalties. 5. **Strengths and weaknesses:** Give your villain distinctive strengths that make them formidable adversaries. It could be intelligence, physical prowess, or an uncanny ability to elude capture. However, also give them weaknesses that the hero and heroine can exploit and use to their advantage. 6. **Memorable appearance:** Consider creating a villain whose appearance reflects their dark nature. It could be a distinctive physical characteristic, such as unique eyes, a scar, or an eerie presence. The way they present themselves can help readers visualize them and add to their sense of menace. 7. **Psychological depth:** Dive into your villain's psyche to explore their twisted thoughts and emotions. This can create a sense of unpredictability and make them truly unsettling.

Conflict and Interaction with Protagonists

The interactions between the villain and the hero and heroine are vital for creating tension and driving the plot forward. The conflict can take many forms, from physical confrontations to psychological mind games. The villain should present a formidable challenge for the protagonists, pushing them to their limits and testing their resolve. Consider these tips for crafting compelling conflicts between villains and protagonists: 1. **Power dynamics:** Explore power struggles between the villain and the hero or heroine. The villain might initially hold the upper hand, compelling the protagonists to find innovative ways to gain the advantage. 2. **Intellectual challenges:** Let the villain engage the protagonists in a battle of wits. This could involve puzzles, riddles, or complex schemes that the heroes must unravel to outsmart the villain. 3. **Emotional manipulation:** Your villain may prey on the emotions and vulnerabilities of the hero and heroine. By exploiting their weaknesses, the villain can create doubt, fear, and internal conflicts that add depth to the story. 4. **Moral dilemmas:** Place the hero and heroine in situations where they have to make difficult choices between what is right and what is necessary to defeat the villain. This creates internal conflict for the protagonists and adds layers of moral complexity to the story. 5. **Parallel character arcs:** Consider giving the villain a character arc that mirrors the hero or heroine's journey. This can heighten the stakes and lead to unexpected twists and revelations.

Conclusion

Creating an unforgettable villain is crucial for a Victorian mystical romance novel. By crafting a complex and charismatic antagonist with believable motivations, strengths, and weaknesses, you will add depth and intensity to the story. The conflict and interactions between the villain and the hero or heroine will drive the plot, captivate readers, and ensure that your novel remains a page-turning exploration of love, mystery, and the supernatural in the Victorian era. Stay tuned for Chapter 29: Reimagining Victorian Myths and Legends. (Note: This chapter can be further expanded with examples and case studies of memorable villains from other Victorian novels or the author's own works.)

Chapter 29: Reimagining Victorian Myths and Legends

In Victorian England, myths and legends held a significant place in the collective imagination. Folktales, legends, and superstitions were often woven into the fabric of daily life, inspiring both fear and fascination. As a writer delving into the realm of mystical romance set in the Victorian era, reimagining these myths and legends can add depth and intrigue to your narrative. Victorian England had its own share of mythical creatures and legends, some originating from ancient folklore and others emerging from the rich imagination of the era. From fairies and ghosts to mermaids and even creatures like Spring-Heeled Jack, the possibilities for reimagining these myths are endless. When reimagining Victorian myths and legends, it is essential to respect the source material while adding your own unique spin. Consider the values and themes associated with these myths and how you can incorporate them into your mystical romance novel. Here are some tips to help you bring these myths to life in a fresh and compelling way: 1. Research and understand the original myths: Before you can reimagine Victorian myths and legends, it is crucial to have a thorough understanding of the original stories. Dive into the rich folklore and fairy tales of the era, immersing yourself in the narratives and symbolism they present. This research will provide a solid foundation for incorporating these elements into your own story. 2. Infuse your own twist: To create a unique and captivating narrative, put your own spin on the myths and legends you are incorporating. Consider how you can add depth to the characters or develop their motivations and conflicts. By reimagining these traditional tales, you have the opportunity to breathe new life into them, captivating readers with unexpected twists and turns. 3. Integrate mythical beings into your story: Bring iconic mythical beings and creatures into your mystical romance novel. Whether it's a mischievous fairy, a vengeful ghost, or an elusive mermaid, explore how these beings can interact with your main characters and shape the course of their journey. Consider their origin, powers, and how they fit into the Victorian society you have created. 4. Explore the symbolism: Victorian myths and legends often carry symbolic meanings. Delve into the themes and symbolism associated with these tales and consider how you can incorporate these deeper meanings into your story. Symbolism can add layers of depth and meaning to your narrative, enhancing the emotional impact of your mystical romance. 5. Craft intricate backstories: Develop intricate backstories for your mythical characters, weaving their origins into the fabric of Victorian society. Consider integrating historical events and societal norms to ground these mythical beings in the reality of the era. By grounding your mythical characters in the historical context, you create a sense of authenticity that will captivate readers. 6. Use myths and legends to drive the plot: Incorporate myths and legends as catalysts for your plot development. Infuse your story with these elements, driving the conflict, creating tension, and intensifying the romantic and mysterious aspects of your novel. Whether it's a quest to uncover the truth about a long-lost myth or a forbidden love between a mortal and a mythical creature, these elements can propel your story forward and keep readers engaged. Remember, the key to reimagining Victorian myths and legends is to stay true to the spirit of the era while adding your own unique twist. By drawing upon these mystical elements, you can create a vibrant and immersive world that will transport readers to the enchanting and mysterious Victorian era. Next up: **Chapter 30: Writing Suspenseful and Thrilling Scenes**

Chapter 30: Writing Suspenseful and Thrilling Scenes

In a Victorian mystical romance novel, suspense and thrill are essential elements that keep readers engaged and on the edge of their seats. These scenes heighten the excitement and create a sense of anticipation as the characters navigate dangerous situations while experiencing the intense emotions of love and magic. Crafting suspenseful and thrilling scenes requires careful attention to pacing, building tension, and creating unexpected twists and turns. Here are some tips to help you master the art of writing suspenseful and thrilling scenes in your Victorian mystical romance novel.

Pace the Scene

The pacing of a scene plays a crucial role in creating suspense and thrill. It's important to control the rhythm of the narrative, alternating between moments of high tension and brief reprieves. Start by establishing a sense of normalcy or tranquility, allowing the readers to feel comfortable before gradually introducing elements of danger or mystery. As the scene progresses, increase the pace by shortening sentences and paragraphs. Utilize action verbs and create a sense of urgency to convey the characters' heightened emotions.

Build Tension

Tension is a key ingredient in creating suspense and thrill in your novel. It keeps readers engaged and eager to find out what happens next. You can build tension by incorporating the following elements:

- Use foreshadowing: Drop subtle hints about impending danger or a hidden threat. This creates an air of anticipation and makes the readers curious about what will happen next.

- Stretch out the suspense: Drag out the moment of revelation or resolution as long as possible. Use descriptive language to heighten the readers' anticipation and keep them on the edge of their seats.
- Show the characters' emotional turmoil: Capture the characters' fear, anxiety, or desperation in vivid detail. This allows readers to empathize with the characters and feel the tension more intensely.
- Use cliffhangers: End chapters or scenes with a dramatic twist or unresolved conflict. This leaves readers craving for closure and wanting to immediately continue reading.

Create Unexpected Twists and Turns

One of the most effective ways to keep readers engaged and thrilled is by introducing unexpected twists and turns. Avoid predictable storylines and clichéd plot devices. Instead, surprise your readers with sudden revelations, shocking betrayals, or unforeseen obstacles that complicate the characters' journey. Keep the readers guessing and constantly challenged. Twists and turns inject excitement and freshness into the narrative, making it difficult for the readers to predict what will happen next and ensuring that they remain invested in the story.

Engage the Senses

Incorporating sensory details is vital for immersing readers in the suspenseful and thrilling scenes of your Victorian mystical romance novel. Engage all the senses to provide a vivid and immersive experience. Describe the eerie silence, the faint whispers in the dark, or the protagonist's pounding heart. Utilize descriptive language to evoke the scents, sounds, and tactile sensations that heighten the tension. The use of sensory imagery will transport readers into the scene and make them feel as if they are right beside the characters, experiencing the danger and thrill firsthand.

Balance Action and Emotion

Suspenseful and thrilling scenes should not only focus on action but also delve into the emotional turmoil of the characters. Explore their fears, doubts, and the intense emotions that arise in challenging situations. By balancing action with emotion, readers will not only be captivated by the physical danger but also emotionally invested in the characters' journey. This balance adds depth and realism to the scenes, making them more impactful and memorable.

Final Thoughts

Writing suspenseful and thrilling scenes is an art that requires careful attention to detail, pacing, and character development. By understanding the principles of building tension, incorporating unexpected twists, engaging the senses, and balancing action and emotion, you can create captivating scenes that keep readers on the edge of their seats. Remember to immerse readers in the perilous world of your Victorian mystical romance novel and leave them eagerly turning the pages to discover the fates of your characters in the face of danger, love, and magic. The Power of Love and Passion: Invoking Emotions in a Victorian Mystical Romance Novel In a Victorian mystical romance novel, the power of love and passion takes center stage. It is through these intense emotions that characters are driven to great lengths, overcoming obstacles, and ultimately finding their happily ever afters. Exploring the power of love and passion adds depth and realism to the story, captivating readers and evoking strong emotions. Love in the Victorian era was considered a powerful force that transcended societal norms and boundaries. It was often portrayed as a force that could conquer all, even in the face of adversity and social barriers. In a mystical romance novel, love can be depicted as magical, fateful, and almost otherworldly. It can bring characters together from different walks of life, unite them against all odds, and even bind them across time and space. Passion, on the other hand, fuels the romance and intensifies the emotional connections between characters. It ignites desire, longing, and a sense of urgency. Passionate moments in a Victorian mystical romance novel can range from stolen glances to heated embraces, from delicate kisses to passionate declarations of love. These moments serve to deepen the emotional bond between characters and engage readers in their journey. To effectively explore the power of love and passion, it is essential to create compelling characters that readers can invest in. Characters should be multidimensional, with their own desires, flaws, and motivations. Their emotions should be authentic and relatable, allowing readers to experience the love and passion alongside them. Dialogue plays a crucial role in showcasing the power of love and passion. It is through heartfelt conversations that characters express their innermost feelings, confess their love, and convey their desires. Dialogue should be infused with emotion, capturing the intensity and vulnerability of the characters' experiences. It should be authentic to the Victorian era, reflecting the language and mannerisms of the time. Furthermore, setting the scene is essential in evoking emotions in a Victorian mystical romance novel. Utilizing descriptive language and imagery, the setting should reflect the characters' emotions and enhance the intensity of their love and passion. Whether it is a moonlit garden, a roaring fireplace, or a secluded hideaway, the setting should evoke a sense of beauty, intimacy, and romanticism. It is also important to create moments of conflict and tension within the romance to heighten the power of love and passion. These obstacles can be internal, such as personal insecurities or conflicting desires, or external, such as societal expectations or meddling individuals. By testing the strength of their love and passion, these challenges serve to intensify the emotions and create a more engaging narrative. When exploring the power of love and passion, it is crucial to balance the intensity with moments of tenderness and vulnerability. These quieter moments allow readers to connect with the characters on a deeper level, sympathizing with their struggles and celebrating their victories. By showcasing the full spectrum of emotions, from passion and desire to tenderness and vulnerability, a Victorian mystical romance novel becomes a truly immersive and emotionally resonant experience for readers. In conclusion, exploring the power of love and passion is a vital aspect of a Victorian mystical romance novel. It is through these intense emotions that characters are driven to overcome obstacles and find their happily ever afters. By creating compelling characters, using authentic dialogue, and crafting evocative settings, authors can capture the full range of emotions and engage readers in a captivating love story that transcends time and boundaries.

Chapter 32: Writing Fateful Endings

In a Victorian mystical romance novel, the ending is a crucial component that leaves a lasting impression on readers. It is the culmination of the characters' journeys, the resolution of conflicts, and the ultimate fulfillment or heartbreak of their destinies. Writing a fateful ending requires careful consideration and attention to detail to create a satisfying conclusion that leaves readers both enchanted and satisfied. Here are some tips for writing fateful endings in a Victorian mystical romance novel: 1. Embrace the Power of Fate: - Bring forth the concept of destiny and the belief that certain events are preordained. - Explore how the characters' choices and actions align with their predetermined fate. - Highlight the idea of love and destiny intertwining, with the idea that true love will ultimately conquer all obstacles. 2. Resolve Conflicts and Tie Loose Ends: - Address all the major conflicts and storylines in the novel. - Ensure that each character's story arc reaches a satisfying resolution. - Tie up any loose ends or unanswered questions to provide closure for readers. 3. Consider the Emotional Impact: - Create emotional depth by allowing characters to face the consequences of their choices. - Explore the full range of emotions, from joy and fulfillment to heartbreak and loss. - Craft moments of vulnerability and reflection for the characters as they come to terms with their fates. 4. Avoid Predictability: - While fateful endings often carry a sense of inevitability, strive to avoid predictability. - Surprise readers with unexpected twists or revelations that add layers of complexity to the conclusion. - Subvert traditional tropes and expectations to keep the ending fresh and engaging. 5. Maintain Authenticity: - Stay true to the Victorian era and the themes established throughout the novel. - Capture the essence of Victorian romance by infusing the ending with passion, longing, and sacrifice. - Consider the social expectations and moral values of the time period, allowing them to inform the characters' choices and the outcome of their fates. 6. Reflect on Themes and Morality: - Revisit the central themes of the novel, such as love, redemption, and the supernatural. - Use the fateful ending to exemplify the moral lessons and values explored throughout the story. - Showcase the growth and transformation of the characters as they learn from their experiences. 7. Balance Closure and Openness: - Provide a sense of closure for readers by addressing the main conflict and character arcs. - Leave room for imagination and speculation by including elements of openness or ambiguity in the ending. - Allow readers to envision the characters' future beyond the pages of the novel. By following these tips, you can create a fateful ending that leaves a lasting impact on readers. Whether it's a happily-ever-after or a bittersweet conclusion, the ending should evoke strong emotions and leave readers pondering the journey of the characters long after they finish the book. Remember to infuse the ending with the unique blend of Victorian romance and mysticism that has captivated readers throughout history.

Chapter 33: Editing and Polishing Your Manuscript

Congratulations! You have completed your Victorian mystical romance novel set in the enchanting world of Marie Corelli. Now comes the important step of editing and polishing your manuscript to ensure it reaches its full potential. In this chapter, we will explore various editing techniques and strategies to help you refine your story and create a polished final product. Editing is a crucial part of the writing process as it allows you to enhance the clarity, coherence, and effectiveness of your storytelling. It involves reviewing your manuscript for errors, inconsistencies, and areas that could be strengthened. Here are some key steps and considerations to keep in mind as you edit and polish your Victorian mystical romance novel: 1. Take a Break: Before diving into the editing process, it is beneficial to take a break from your manuscript. Stepping away for a few days or even weeks will give you a fresh perspective and make it easier to identify areas that need improvement. 2. Revise for Structure and Flow: Start by evaluating the overall structure and flow of your story. Does it have a clear beginning, middle, and end? Are there any gaps in the plot or pacing issues? Make necessary revisions to ensure your story flows smoothly and engages readers from start to finish. 3. Strengthen Characters and Dialogue: Pay close attention to your characters' development and dialogue. Are your characters well-rounded and relatable? Do their actions and words align with their personalities and motivations? Revise and refine dialogue to make it natural and engaging. 4. Enhance Descriptions and Imagery: Victorian mystical romance novels thrive on vivid descriptions and evocative imagery. Ensure your descriptions are rich and immersive, allowing readers to visualize the setting, characters, and magical elements of your story. Use sensory details to create a multisensory experience for your readers. 5. Eliminate Unnecessary Details: While details are important, it's crucial to strike a balance and avoid overwhelming readers with too much information. Remove any unnecessary details that do not serve the plot, character development, or the overall atmosphere. 6. Check for Consistency: Consistency is key when it comes to creating a believable world for your readers. Double-check names, dates, locations, and any other elements that should remain consistent throughout your novel. Ensure that your characters' traits, appearances, and backstories are consistent as well. 7. Polish Grammar and Punctuation: Pay attention to grammar, punctuation, and sentence structure. Edit for clarity and readability, removing any ambiguous or convoluted sentences. Thoroughly proofread your manuscript for typos, spelling errors, and grammar mistakes. Consider using professional editing tools or hiring a professional editor to ensure accuracy. 8. Seek Feedback: Once you have gone through several rounds of editing and polishing, it's helpful to seek feedback from beta readers, writing groups, or even professional editors. They can offer fresh perspectives and identify areas that may need further improvement. 9. Fine-Tuning: After incorporating feedback, take the time to fine-tune your manuscript. Focus on specific areas that require extra attention, such as dialogue, pacing, or character development. Polish sentences and paragraphs to ensure clarity and coherence. 10. Final Proofreading: Before considering your manuscript complete, perform a final proofread to catch any lingering errors or inconsistencies. Read your novel aloud, as it can help you notice awkward phrasing or rhythm. Alternatively, consider having someone else proofread your manuscript for a fresh pair of eyes. Remember, the editing process is iterative, and it may take several rounds to achieve the desired result. Approach the editing process with patience, a critical eye, and a willingness to revise and improve your work. By thoroughly editing and polishing your Victorian mystical romance novel, you can create a captivating and professional book that will enchant readers. Good luck!

Chapter 34: Finding an Agent and Publishing Your Book

Publishing a Victorian mystical romance novel requires navigating the world of literary agents and publishers. Finding the right agent and securing a publishing deal can be a daunting process, but with careful research and preparation, it is achievable. In this chapter, we will explore the steps involved in finding an agent and publishing your book.

The Role of a Literary Agent

A literary agent serves as a bridge between authors and publishers. They represent authors and their works, negotiate book deals, and provide guidance throughout the publishing process. Having a literary agent can significantly increase your chances of securing a publishing contract and navigating the complex world of publishing.

Researching Literary Agents

Before approaching literary agents, it is essential to do thorough research. Look for agents who specialize in your genre, specifically Victorian mystical romance. Study their client list, track record, and submission guidelines. Use resources like online databases, industry websites, and writer's associations to find reputable agents.

Preparing Your Submission Package

Once you have identified a list of potential agents, it's time to prepare your submission package. This typically includes: 1. Query letter: A well-crafted query letter is crucial in grabbing an agent's attention. It should introduce your novel, provide a brief synopsis, and highlight your writing credentials or relevant experience. 2. Synopsis: A concise summary of your novel that outlines the main plot points, including the central conflict, resolution, and character arcs. Keep it engaging and free of major spoilers. 3. Sample chapters: Literary agents often request a sample of your writing to assess your skill and style. Choose a few compelling chapters or a significant portion of your novel that showcases your best work. 4. Author bio: Include a brief biography that highlights your writing experience, any awards or accolades, and relevant credentials or expertise.

Submitting to Agents

Follow the submission guidelines provided by each agent. Some prefer email submissions, while others may require physical mail. Pay attention to specific formatting, document length, and any additional materials requested. Personalize each submission by addressing the agent by name and referencing why you believe they would be a good fit for your work. Avoid generic queries and show that you have done your research on their agency and client list.

Understanding the Querying Process

After submitting your query, it's important to be patient. Agents receive numerous queries daily, and the process can take several weeks or even months. Some agents may request partial or full manuscripts, while others may decline your submission. Rejections are a normal part of the process, so don't be discouraged.

Traditional Publishing vs. Self-Publishing

When it comes to publishing your Victorian mystical romance novel, you have two main options: traditional publishing or self-publishing. Traditional publishing involves signing a contract with a publishing house. They handle editing, cover design, distribution, and marketing. However, it can be a competitive and lengthy process, often requiring multiple rejections before finding a publisher. Self-publishing gives you full control over the publishing process. You are responsible for editing, cover design, formatting, and marketing. Self-published authors often use online platforms like Amazon Kindle Direct Publishing (KDP) or Smashwords to distribute their books. It offers flexibility and higher royalties but requires more extensive self-promotion.

Choosing the Right Path for Your Book

Consider your goals, budget, and time commitments when deciding between traditional publishing and self-publishing. Traditional publishing may offer wider distribution and access to professional resources but may take longer. Self-publishing provides more control over the process but requires a greater investment of time and effort in marketing and promotion.

Marketing and Promoting Your Book

Regardless of the publishing path you choose, marketing and promoting your Victorian mystical romance novel are crucial for success. Build an author platform by creating a professional website or blog, engaging on social media, and connecting with your target audience. Consider participating in book signings, literary events, and conferences to network with readers and industry professionals. Guest blogging, securing book reviews, and running online promotions can also boost visibility.

Connecting with Readers in the Digital Age

In today's digital age, connecting with readers has become easier through social media, book blogs, author newsletters, and online book clubs. Leverage these platforms to engage with your readers, build a loyal fan base, and increase your book's visibility. Remember to engage in meaningful discussions, share behind-the-scenes insights, and create content that resonates with your target audience. Building relationships with readers can lead to valuable word-of-mouth recommendations and long-term success.

Conclusion

Finding an agent and navigating the publishing process is an exciting and sometimes challenging journey. By conducting thorough research, crafting compelling submission materials, and actively participating in the marketing and promotion of your book, you increase your chances of success as a Victorian mystical romance author. Embrace the process, continue honing your craft, and strive to create captivating stories that transport readers to the enchanting world of the Victorian era. Now that you have a better understanding of finding an agent and publishing your book, let's move on to Chapter 35: Marketing and Promoting Your Victorian Romance Novel.

Chapter 35: Marketing and Promoting Your Victorian Romance Novel

In Chapter 35 of "The Victorian Lady's Guide to Researching and Writing a Mystical Romance Novel in the Style of Marie Corelli," we will delve into the essential aspects of marketing and promoting your Victorian romance novel. Writing a captivating story filled with love and magic is just the first step; now it's time to ensure that your book reaches its intended audience and generates the interest it deserves.

Developing a Marketing Plan

To effectively market your Victorian romance novel, you need a well-thought-out plan. Begin by identifying your target audience, researching their reading habits, and determining where and how you can reach them. Consider the following key elements:

Book Cover and Design

The first impression your book makes is through its cover and design. Capture the essence of your Victorian romance novel by working with a talented cover designer who can help create a visually appealing and evocative cover. Pay attention to typography, color schemes, and imagery that reflect the themes and atmosphere of your story.

Book Description and Blurbs

Your book description plays a crucial role in enticing potential readers. Craft a compelling synopsis that highlights the unique elements of your Victorian romance novel and leaves readers eager to delve into its pages. Additionally, seek endorsements from established authors or influencers within the genre to provide compelling blurbs that can be displayed on your book's cover or in promotional materials.

Online Presence and Author Website

In today's digital age, having a strong online presence is crucial for promoting your book. Create an author website where readers can learn more about you and your Victorian romance novels. Use this platform to share updates, provide background information on your research process, and engage with your readers through blog posts or newsletters.

Social Media Marketing

Utilize social media platforms such as Facebook, Instagram, Twitter, and Goodreads to connect with potential readers and promote your Victorian romance novel. Engage with your audience, share relevant content, host giveaways, and collaborate with other authors or book bloggers to expand your reach.

Book Launch Strategies

Plan a memorable book launch event to generate excitement and engage with your readers directly. Consider hosting a virtual launch through platforms like Zoom or organizing a physical event at a local bookstore or venue. Offer special incentives such as signed copies, exclusive merchandise, or themed giveaways to incentivize attendance and increase interest in your novel.

Collaborating with Influencers and Book Bloggers

Partnering with influencers and book bloggers who specialize in romance novels or the Victorian era can help amplify your book's visibility. Reach out to these individuals with personalized pitches, offering them free copies of your novel or hosting interviews or guest blog posts on their platforms. Their endorsements and reviews can greatly impact your book's success.

Book Reviews and Reader Engagement

Encourage readers to leave reviews on platforms like Amazon, Goodreads, or BookBub once they've finished your novel. Positive reviews not only boost your book's credibility but also attract new readers. Engage with your readers by responding to comments and messages, and consider hosting Q&A sessions or virtual book clubs to foster a sense of community and deepen reader engagement.

Bookstore and Library Outreach

Approach local independent bookstores and libraries to see if they would be interested in carrying your Victorian romance novel. Offer to participate in author events, signings, or readings to attract potential readers. Consider partnering with libraries to host historical talks or workshops related to the Victorian era, positioning yourself as an expert in the genre.

Utilizing Book Promotion Platforms

Explore book promotion platforms such as BookBub, BookSweeps, or eBookDaily, which can help you reach a wider audience by featuring your novel in their newsletters or on their websites. Research and choose platforms tailored to the historical romance genre to maximize exposure.

Continuing Marketing Efforts

Remember that marketing and promotion are ongoing processes that require consistent effort and adaptation. Monitor the results of your marketing strategies, track sales, and adjust your approach accordingly. Stay up to date with industry trends, attend book fairs or conferences, and network with other authors and professionals to expand your knowledge and opportunities. By implementing these marketing and promotional strategies, you can increase the visibility and success of your Victorian romance novel. Embrace the opportunity to connect with readers who appreciate the passion, magic, and mystique of the Victorian era, ultimately ensuring the longevity of your writing career.

Chapter 36: Connecting with Readers in the Digital Age

The digital age has brought about significant changes in the way writers connect with their readers. With the advent of technology and the rise of social media, authors now have more opportunities than ever to engage with their audience and create a lasting relationship. This chapter will explore various strategies for connecting with readers in the digital age and building a loyal fan base for your Victorian mystical romance novel.

1. Establish a strong online presence

To connect with readers in the digital age, it is important to establish a strong online presence. This can be done through various platforms such as a website, blog, and social media channels. Create a professional website where readers can learn more about you and your work. Include information about your Victorian mystical romance novel, your inspirations, and any upcoming events or releases. In addition to your website, consider starting a blog where you can share behind-the-scenes insights into your writing process, historical research, and updates on your upcoming projects. This will not only engage your existing readers but also attract potential new readers who are interested in Victorian-era romance novels. Social media platforms such as Facebook, Instagram, Twitter, and Goodreads are also great tools for connecting with readers. Regularly post updates about your writing progress, share interesting facts or quotes from your novel, and interact with your followers. Respond to comments and messages in a timely manner, and show genuine interest in your readers' feedback and opinions.

2. Engage with your readers

Connecting with readers goes beyond just having an online presence. Actively engaging with your readers is crucial to building a strong and dedicated fan base. Responding to comments and messages on social media, participating in book clubs or reading groups, and attending book signings and author events are all great ways to engage with your readers. Consider hosting live Q&A sessions on platforms like Facebook Live or Instagram Live, where readers can ask you questions directly. This not only allows you to connect with your readers on a personal level but also gives them a sense of exclusivity and access to the author behind the book. Another way to engage with readers is by offering exclusive content or rewards. This could be bonus chapters, short stories, or even personalized bookplates for those who pre-order your novel. By providing these incentives, you are not only showing your appreciation for your readers' support but also deepening their connection with your work.

3. Build a community

Building a community of readers who share a love for Victorian mystical romance novels can be a powerful way to connect with your audience. Consider creating a Facebook group or an online forum where readers can discuss your book, ask questions, and interact with one another. Within this community, you can also create opportunities for readers to become brand ambassadors or beta readers. By involving them in the early stages of your writing process, you not only make them feel valued but also gain valuable feedback for future novels. Hosting virtual book clubs or participating in online book discussions can also strengthen the sense of community among your readers. This not only fosters engagement but also provides an opportunity for readers to connect with one another and share their thoughts and interpretations of your Victorian mystical romance novel.

4. Collaborate with influencers and bloggers

Working with influencers and bloggers who have a strong following in the Victorian romance genre can help expand your reach and connect with new readers. Identify popular book bloggers or influencers who specialize in Victorian-era literature and reach out to them. Offer them a review copy of your novel or ask if they would be interested in hosting an author interview or guest post on their platforms. Collaborating with influencers and bloggers not only helps to generate buzz around your Victorian mystical romance novel but also exposes your work to a wider audience who may become potential readers and fans. The key is to find influencers who align with your target audience and have an engaged and genuine following.

5. Utilize email marketing

Email marketing is a powerful tool for connecting with readers and keeping them engaged. Offer readers the opportunity to sign up for your newsletter on your website or social media platforms. Regularly send out newsletters with updates on your writing progress, exclusive content, and behind-the-scenes insights. In your newsletters, consider including interactive elements such as polls or surveys to encourage readers to participate and share their thoughts. This not only helps you gain valuable feedback but also creates a sense of community and involvement.

Conclusion

In the digital age, connecting with readers has never been more accessible and important for authors. By establishing a strong online presence, engaging with your readers, building a community, collaborating with influencers, and utilizing email marketing, you can create a lasting connection with your audience and nurture a loyal fan base for your Victorian mystical romance novel. Embrace the opportunities that the digital age provides and continue to engage with your readers to create a meaningful and immersive reading experience.

Chapter 37: Overcoming Writer's Block and Self-Doubt

As a writer, experiencing periods of writer's block and self-doubt is not uncommon. These creative roadblocks can hinder progress and leave you feeling frustrated, demotivated, and uncertain about your abilities. In this chapter, we will explore strategies and techniques to overcome writer's block and self-doubt, allowing you to continue writing your Victorian mystical romance novel with confidence and inspiration.

Understanding Writer's Block

Writer's block refers to a state of being unable to produce new work or feeling stuck in the writing process. It can manifest as a complete lack of ideas, difficulty in developing a plot, or struggling to find the right words. Writer's block can be caused by various factors, including stress, burnout, fear of failure, perfectionism, or a lack of inspiration.

Identifying the Root Cause

The first step in overcoming writer's block is to identify the underlying cause. Reflect on your current mindset and emotions. Are you feeling overwhelmed? Are you putting too much pressure on yourself? Are you afraid of not meeting expectations? By pinpointing the root cause, you can address it directly and develop a plan to move past it.

Breaking the Routine

Sometimes, writer's block can be a result of falling into a monotonous routine. Consider shaking up your writing habits. Experiment with different writing locations, change your writing time, or try writing with pen and paper instead of a computer. Exploring new environments and methods can stimulate creativity and get the words flowing.

Seeking Inspiration

When you're feeling creatively blocked, seeking inspiration can help reignite your imagination. Read books in the same genre as your Victorian mystical romance novel to gather ideas, explore new topics, or even delve into different mediums like paintings or music. Inspiration can be found in the most unexpected places, so keep an open mind and actively engage with art, literature, and the world around you.

Setting Realistic Goals

Setting realistic writing goals is essential in overcoming writer's block. Break down your novel into smaller, manageable tasks. Instead of focusing on completing the entire book, dedicate your attention to writing a specific chapter, scene, or even a single paragraph. By setting achievable goals, you will experience a sense of accomplishment, which can reignite your motivation and confidence.

Overcoming Self-Doubt

Self-doubt is a common obstacle that many writers face. It stems from a lack of confidence in your abilities and a fear of judgment or rejection. Overcoming self-doubt is crucial in order to fully express your creativity and write with conviction. Here are some strategies to help you overcome self-doubt:

Positive Self-Talk

Challenge the negative thoughts and self-criticisms by replacing them with positive affirmations. Remind yourself of your past achievements, acknowledge your growth as a writer, and believe in your ability to create a captivating Victorian mystical romance novel. Surround yourself with positive influences and support systems that uplift and encourage you.

Embrace Imperfections

Perfectionism can be a major source of self-doubt. Remember that writing is a process, and no first draft is flawless. Embrace the imperfections and understand that revision and editing are natural parts of the writing journey. Allow yourself to make mistakes and view them as opportunities for growth and improvement.

Celebrate Small Victories

Recognize and celebrate your accomplishments, no matter how small they may seem. Completing a chapter, receiving positive feedback from beta readers, or simply meeting your writing goals for the day are all steps forward in your writing journey. By celebrating these small victories, you reinforce your belief in yourself and your abilities.

Find a Supportive Community

Join writing groups, interact with fellow authors, and seek out mentors or writing partners who can provide guidance and support. Surrounding yourself with like-minded individuals who understand the challenges of writing can help boost your confidence and provide reassurance during moments of self-doubt.

Practicing Self-Care

Taking care of yourself physically, mentally, and emotionally is vital in overcoming self-doubt. Prioritize self-care activities that help you relax, recharge, and refocus. Engage in activities that bring you joy, such as practicing mindfulness, exercising, spending time in nature, or pursuing other creative interests. Remember that your well-being is crucial to your writing success.

Conclusion

Writer's block and self-doubt are common obstacles that writers face, but they don't have to define your writing journey. By understanding and addressing the root causes of writer's block, seeking inspiration, setting realistic goals, and adopting strategies to overcome self-doubt, you can break through these barriers and continue writing your Victorian mystical romance novel with renewed enthusiasm and confidence. Embrace the process, stay committed, and remember that your unique voice and story deserve to be shared with the world.

Chapter 38: Building a Writing Routine and Staying Inspired

As a writer, establishing a writing routine is crucial for maintaining discipline and consistency in your craft. A routine helps create a dedicated time and space for writing, allowing you to focus and stay on track with your goals. Building a writing routine not only enhances your productivity but also helps to nurture your creativity.

Creating a Writing Schedule

To build an effective writing routine, start by creating a writing schedule that works best for you. Consider your daily commitments and identify blocks of time when you can dedicate solely to writing. It could be early in the morning, during lunch breaks, or in the evenings. Find a time when you feel most energized and focused, as it can significantly impact your writing productivity.

Setting Writing Goals

Setting writing goals is essential for maintaining motivation and measuring your progress. Determine the word count or page count you want to achieve each writing session or establish weekly or monthly writing targets. Breaking down your writing goals into smaller, more manageable tasks can make them feel less overwhelming and more achievable.

Creating a Writing Space

Having a designated writing space can help you get into the right mindset and minimize distractions. It could be a separate room in your house, a cozy corner in a coffee shop, or a quiet corner in a library.

Ensure that your writing space is free of clutter and equipped with the necessary writing tools, such as a comfortable chair, a desk, and a computer or notebook.

Finding Inspiration

To stay inspired, surround yourself with sources of inspiration. This could include reading books in your genre, studying the works of Victorian authors, researching historical events, or exploring the natural world. Visiting museums, attending writing conferences, or joining writing groups can also provide new ideas and perspectives.

Developing Writing Rituals

Incorporating writing rituals into your routine can help signal your brain that it's time to focus and be creative. It could involve lighting a scented candle, brewing a cup of tea or coffee, putting on soft instrumental music, or taking a short walk before sitting down to write. Consistently repeating these rituals can train your brain to switch into writing mode and boost your creativity.

Taking Breaks

Taking breaks is essential for avoiding burnout and rejuvenating your creative energy. During your writing routine, make sure to take regular breaks to rest, stretch, and recharge. Engage in activities that inspire you and allow your mind to relax, such as going for a walk, practicing mindfulness, or engaging in a hobby unrelated to writing. These breaks can help you come back to your writing with fresh ideas and a renewed enthusiasm.

Overcoming Writer's Block

Writer's block can be a common challenge, but there are strategies to overcome it. If you find yourself stuck, try freewriting, where you write spontaneously without worrying about grammar or structure. You can also switch to a different writing project or work on a different aspect of your current story, such as character development or outlining. Additionally, seeking support from other writers or participating in writing exercises and prompts can help stimulate your creativity and break through the block.

Staying Accountable

Accountability is crucial for sticking to your writing routine. Consider finding a writing accountability partner or joining a writing group where you can share your goals and progress. Having someone to hold you accountable can motivate you to stay consistent and focused on your writing goals.

Adapting and Flexibility

While a routine is important, it's also essential to remain flexible and adaptable. Life can throw unexpected challenges your way, and it's important to adjust your writing routine accordingly. Be open to change and find alternatives when your regular writing schedule is disrupted. Remember, the goal is to keep writing consistently, even if it means adjusting your routine temporarily.

Conclusion

Building a writing routine is crucial for staying committed to your writing craft and maintaining consistency. By creating a writing schedule, setting goals, finding inspiration, developing rituals, taking breaks, and staying accountable, you can establish a routine that supports your creative process and helps you stay inspired and motivated. Embrace the routine while remaining flexible, and remember that writing is a journey of self-discovery and growth.

Chapter 39: Continuing the Victorian Literary Tradition

Victorian literature holds a special place in the hearts of readers even today. The works of authors like Charles Dickens, Charlotte Brontë, and Elizabeth Gaskell have left an indelible mark on the literary landscape. In this chapter, we will explore how you can continue the Victorian literary tradition in your mystical romance novel.

Understanding the Victorian Literary Tradition

The Victorian era was known for its rich and diverse literary output. From sensational novels to social commentaries, Victorian writers explored a wide range of themes and genres. Their works reflected the societal changes of the time, including the class divide, industrialization, and women's rights. To continue the Victorian literary tradition in your mystical romance novel, it is important to understand the characteristics of Victorian literature. Here are a few key elements to consider:

Social Realism

Victorian literature often depicted the harsh realities of social inequality and the plight of the working class. Explore social issues in your novel, shedding light on the struggles and triumphs of characters from different social backgrounds. Use your mystical elements to enhance and emphasize these themes.

Moral Themes

Victorian literature was typically infused with moral and ethical dilemmas. Explore the moral choices faced by your characters and the consequences of their actions. Consider the impact of love and magic on their moral compass and how these elements can lead to redemption or moral enlightenment.

Detailed Descriptions

Victorian writers were known for their descriptive prose, painting detailed and vivid pictures of the settings, characters, and emotions. Transport your readers to the Victorian era by using rich and evocative language to describe the architecture, fashion, and atmosphere of the time.

Embracing the Victorian Style

While continuing the Victorian literary tradition, it is important to develop your own unique voice and style. However, you can incorporate elements of the Victorian writing style to create an immersive reading experience.

Ornate Language

Victorian literature often featured elaborate and flowery language. Embrace this style by using poetic language and vivid imagery. Create a romantic and mystical atmosphere through your choice of words and descriptive metaphors.

Multi-layered Narratives

Victorian novels were known for their complex narratives and intertwining plotlines. Incorporate multiple storylines and subplots in your mystical romance novel to add depth and intrigue. Weave together themes of love, magic, destiny, and societal issues to create a multi-layered narrative that captivates readers.

Character Development

Victorian literature placed a strong emphasis on character development. Take the time to delve deep into your characters' backgrounds, motivations, and inner conflicts. Develop complex and multidimensional characters that readers can connect with on an emotional level.

Contributing to the Victorian Literary Canon

As you continue the Victorian literary tradition in your mystical romance novel, remember that you are part of a rich and storied canon. Pay homage to the Victorian authors who paved the way for your own literary journey while simultaneously bringing a fresh perspective to the genre. By incorporating social realism, moral themes, and detailed descriptions, you can create a novel that resonates with readers and pays tribute to the Victorian era. Embrace the ornate language and multi-layered narratives of the Victorian style while putting your own unique spin on them. Continue the legacy of Victorian literature by crafting a mystical romance novel that transports readers to the enchanting world of the past while exploring timeless themes of love, fate, and redemption. Next, in Chapter 40, we will explore the intricacies of writing a series and expanding your mystical romance world.

Chapter 40: Writing a Series: Expanding Your Mystical Romance World

Writing a series of books can be an exciting and challenging endeavor, especially when it comes to expanding your mystical romance world. In this chapter, we will explore how to continue the story and engage readers by creating a captivating series.

The Benefits of Writing a Series

Writing a series has numerous benefits for both authors and readers. For authors, it allows for further exploration of the world and characters they have created, providing the opportunity to delve deeper into their stories. It also helps to build a loyal fan base and increase book sales. Readers, on the other hand, enjoy the chance to revisit beloved characters, uncover new mysteries, and immerse themselves in a familiar and enchanting world.

Mapping Out Your Series

Before diving into writing a series, it's important to consider the overall arc of the story. Begin by outlining the main plot points and character arcs for each book in the series. This will provide a roadmap to guide your writing and ensure consistency throughout the series. Consider how the mystical elements and romance will evolve over the course of the books, and how each installment will build upon the previous ones.

Developing New Characters and Relationships

As you expand your mystical romance world, it's essential to introduce new and compelling characters. These characters can add depth and complexity to the story, creating new relationships and conflicts for your existing characters. Be sure to give your new additions their own unique qualities, motivations, and backstories. Additionally, consider the dynamic between the new characters and the established ones, allowing for growth and development within the series.

Advancing the Mystery and Romance

In a series, it's crucial to keep readers engaged and invested in the ongoing mystery and romance. While closure is important at the end of each book, leave open-ended questions or lingering threads that can be explored in future installments. Advance the central romance by deepening the emotional connection between the main characters, introducing new challenges and obstacles, and developing their relationship over time. Similarly, continue to unravel the overarching mystery, revealing new twists and revelations that will captivate readers and keep them eagerly turning the pages.

Balancing Familiarity and Freshness

When writing a series, it is important to strike a balance between familiarity and freshness. While readers enjoy revisiting familiar settings and characters, it is equally important to introduce new elements that will keep the story and world intriguing. This can be achieved through new mystical elements, unexpected plot twists, or by exploring previously unexplored aspects of the world. By striking this balance, you can satisfy your readers' desire for familiarity while still providing them with new and exciting experiences.

Maintaining Continuity and Consistency

Maintaining continuity and consistency across a series is essential to ensure a seamless reading experience for your audience. Keep a series bible or detailed notes to track important details such as character attributes, locations, and plot points. Consistently refer back to these notes to avoid any discrepancies or contradictions in later books. Additionally, pay close attention to character development and ensure that the growth and changes they experience throughout the series are authentic and believable.

Evolving as an Author

Writing a series offers the opportunity for personal growth and development as an author. As you progress through the series, take note of reader feedback and reviews to refine and improve your storytelling skills. Embrace the opportunity to experiment with different narrative techniques, character arcs, and plot structures. With each installment, you have the chance to hone your craft and create a more immersive and captivating mystical romance world.

Conclusion

Expanding your mystical romance world through a series allows for deeper exploration of characters, relationships, and the intricate web of magic and romance. By carefully mapping out your series, developing new characters, advancing the mystery and romance, balancing familiarity and freshness, maintaining continuity, and evolving as an author, you can create a series that enchants readers and leaves them eagerly awaiting the next installment. So grab your pen and let your imagination soar as you embark on this exciting journey of writing a mystical romance series.

Don't miss out!

Visit the website below and you can sign up to receive emails whenever Aster Alderdice publishes a new book. There's no charge and no obligation.

https://books2read.com/r/B-A-PWKAB-DTBOC

BOOKS 2 READ

Connecting independent readers to independent writers.

Did you love *The Victorian Lady's Guide to Researching and Writing a Mystical Romance Novel in the Style of Marie Corelli*? Then you should read *An Inheritance of Love*[1] by Aster Alderdice!

[2]

Celebrate the enduring power of love in the heart of rural Scotland with 'An Inheritance of Love.' Follow the lifelong journey of Sir William Sinclair and Lady Genevieve Thorne as their love story weaves through the seasons, embracing the beauty of the Scottish countryside and transcending the tests of time. From their chance encounter as children to their enduring love in old age, their tale is a pledge to the resilience of the human spirit and the timeless beauty of a love that knows no bounds

---

1. https://books2read.com/u/brBMdw

2. https://books2read.com/u/brBMdw

About the Author

Adoring Souls will coddle their hearts with these love embers from Victorian highlands, heath and woods. The sweetness of violet sugar sometimes enters by way of fae and wisps. Take pleasure in the country fireside.

9 798223 711131